SHOOTING STAR

G·K
Hall
&Co.

Also published in Large Print
from G.K. Hall by Brock & Bodie Thoene:

In My Father's House
A Thousand Shall Fall

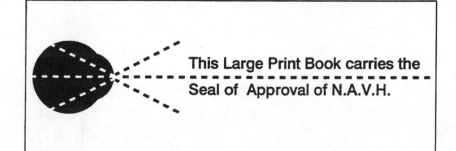

This Large Print Book carries the
Seal of Approval of N.A.V.H.

SHOOTING STAR

☆ ☆ ☆ ☆ ☆ ☆

Brock & Bodie Thoene

G.K. Hall & Co.
Thorndike, Maine

G.K. Hall Large Print Inspirational Collection.

Published in 1994 by arrangement with Bethany House Publishers.

The text of this Large Print edition is unabridged.
Other aspects of the book may vary from the original edition.

Set in 16 pt. News Plantin by Melissa Harvey.

Printed in the United States on acid-free, high opacity paper. ∞

Library of Congress Cataloging in Publication Data

Thoene, Brock, 1952–
    Shooting star / Brock & Bodie Thoene.
      p.   cm.
    ISBN 0-8161-5908-4 (alk. paper : lg. print)
    1. Frontier and pioneer life — Sierra Nevada
(Calif. and Nev.) — Fiction. 2. Large type books.
    I. Thoene, Bodie, 1951– . II. Title.
    [PS3570.H463S48 1994]
    813'.54—dc20   93-33578

"For the great-grandson of
Andrew Jackson Sinnickson —
H.T. (Tommy) Turner

— with love and thanks —"

PROLOGUE[*]

Shiloh, Arkansas
September 24, 1910

The gold case of the old Rockford pocket watch lay open beside the huge stack of manuscript pages heaped on the old man's desk. Soft ticking provided a gentle rhythm behind the urgent scratching of pen against notepaper. The thin golden watch hands swept across the ivory face, as if to remind the writer that time was passing too quickly for him. Time was running out. Only a thousand pages of his life had been written, and surely it would take ten thousand more to tell the whole story!

He paused and glared at the watch. No. It was not the timepiece that was the enemy but *Time.* . . . The old man cocked a bushy eyebrow and tugged his drooping mustache as he recalled how he had come to carry the watch and the heavy gold watch chain and the California-minted ten-dollar gold-piece watch fob. It was a tale the children never tired of hearing. One of their favorites, and yet the old man had not yet put the story down on paper. He held off writing it as though

---

[*]As taken from the Prologue to *A Thousand Shall Fall.*

7

he could bribe the watch and slow down the steady forward movement of its hands. *"And when I've written about you, old friend,"* he often whispered to the timepiece, *"then I'll shut your golden case and send you to Jim to carry. I shall lay down my pen at last, and you may mark the hour of my passing as just another tick of your cycle."*

But the watch made no promise in return, as though it did not care if the story of pocket watch and chain and fob were ever written.

But there were other tales to tell. The dark eyes of the old man flitted to the black fist-sized stone paperweight that prevented the wind from scattering the legacy in the heap of papers before him.

It was the story of this stone that the old man now struggled to recount. The most important story of his eighty-six years was in that hunk of iron and nickel! It had saved his life when he was twenty-six years old. It had given him the gift of sixty more years to live. It had made possible the sons and a daughter and grandsons to gather at his knee and beg, *"Tell us the story of the star, Grandpa Sinnickson! Tell it again!"*

For sixty years he had hefted up the stone and cried, *"Well now, boys! Listen up! This may look like just a black rock to you, but it's more than that! It ain't gold, but it's more than gold! This ain't an ordinary stone, no sir! This is a star! Yessir, boys! You heard me right! A star! Straight from heaven it came, blazing across the sky on the darkest night of my life! With a tail of fire a mile long, it screamed down to earth and saved my life in a most miraculous way! Listen up now, boys, and I'll tell you about it. For it is the truth, and I stand alive here as witness to it!"* And then they would pass the star from hand to hand. The eyes of young and old grew wide at the story of danger and death and the miracle of the falling star.

Perhaps of all the stories, this was the most often repeated. This was the most important tale to be written down because *it made all the rest of his life possible. . . .*

The high shrill cry of the Hartford train echoed across the valley of Shiloh, interrupting his reverie. The old man peered at the watch a moment.

"Late again," he grumbled, snatching up the timepiece and striding to part the curtains of his bedroom window.

Just above the golden tops of the autumn trees, a dark gray plume marked the progress of the locomotive. Far across the valley the tall straight row of birch trees trembled and swayed as if to bow toward the train.

"The boys are playing in the trees again," the old man muttered. Glancing at his watch again, he whispered a warning, "You're late, boys. Get on down. Get home before your father gets wind you're having a good time. Hurry home now, boys!"

As if they heard his distant heart, the two small boys in the birch trees began their descent. Bending the slender trunks low, they rode the treetops to the ground and tumbled onto the field.

The old man mopped his brow in relief as he

watched the two red-shirted figures dash up the hill toward home. Perhaps their father, who had no timepiece, would not know they were late.

For a long time the old man stood at the window and stared across the dusky fields at the birch trees. He had planted those trees with his own hands. A tall straight row of birch trees for his grandsons to climb and ride. Too bad their father did not believe that small boys were created to climb and whoop and laugh. . . .

Sam Tucker would leave a legacy of harshness, of distance and cruelty, for his sons. It was for this reason that their grandpa, the old man, worked day and night on the tales of his own life.

Clicking the watch face closed, he turned from the window and returned to his task. Filling his pen with ink, he tapped the nib on the blotter. It was easier to tell the story aloud than it was to put it down on silent paper, and so he whispered the words as he wrote at the top of the page. . . .

To Grandson Birch
from
Grandfather Andrew Jackson Sinnickson:

Already I have written one thousand pages, and yet I find I have come only to my twenty-sixth year. This may yet be the most important tale of all my legacy, however, as in it I learned by the miracle of a falling star how God delivers those who trust Him. Read on, Birch, for it is a story you seem not to tire of. Perhaps one day you will have sons of your own you may read these words to. Then you will tell them early what I have learned late: 'A thousand shall fall at thy side and ten thousand at thy right hand, but it shall not come nigh thee . . .'

September 24, 1910

CHAPTER 1

Jack Powers. Now there is a name to frighten children into behaving. "Straighten up!" the Californio mothers would say, "or Jack Powers will get you!"

Long before Joaquin Murrieta rode into legend on a flashy stallion named Revenge, and much earlier than Black Bart ever penned his first poem, Powers was well known and feared. From the southern California cantinas of the City of the Angels, to the miners' hovels of Angel's Camp in the Sierras, Powers had a name as the genuine article: the first and worst of the California bad men.

I first crossed trails with Powers in the sleepy sunlit presidio town of Santa Barbara. Powers was a sergeant in Stevenson's regiment — New York boys they were — sent to garrison Santa Barbara against rebellion in the spring of '47. They were a crude, cutthroat band right from the beginning. Recruited straight out of Hell's Kitchen and the Bowery, the regiment drank their enlistment bonus and did not sober up till they were a day and a night out of New York Harbor.

By the time the stinking tub of a transport dropped her hook off the point, the toughs of Company F had had three and a half months of hard tack and green salt beef to regret their decision

13

to enlist. They came ashore sober, angry and spoiling for drink and fight. Powers was the worst, because he intended to give them plenty of both and make a profit in the doing.

Sergeant Jack Powers was supposed to be in charge of discipline for Company F. That's like setting a diamond-back rattler to ride herd on a nest of sidewinders. Within a week of Company F's arrival, there were two dozen new cantinas selling rotgut liquor to the soldiers. Within two weeks, every one of them was paying extortion money to Powers. This added cost of doing business, the cantina owners reasoned, was better than having their places burned, as happened to two who resisted, or being found floating face down in the ocean off Goleta, as with a third.

For all that, I might still have avoided tangling with Powers if I had not volunteered to accompany Will Reed's cook, Simona, into town that fine April morning.

My paint mare, Shawnee, was stepping out right smart, enjoying the feel of the salt breeze off the big water. I had to hold her in check to keep from outpacing the squawking and groaning oxcart. "Simona," I said, "haven't you got any way to make that beast go faster?"

"No, Señor Andrew," she said, "but the cabestro will move no slower either, and he always gets where he is going."

She added a comment about how this ox could find his way to and from town without any guidance, but her words were almost lost in the most frightful wail yet from the solid wood wheels.

"Don't you folks ever grease those wheels?" I asked.

"*Sí*," she said, "but you can hear Señor Carreta asking for more."

"What do you mean?"

"Listen, señor," Simona said with a straight face. "He says, 'Quiero sebo, quiero sebo.' " Her words were a perfect mimic of the high-pitched squawk of the cart. "I want tallow, I want tallow," and she laughed right in my face.

Well, I got to laughing too — the sort of laugh that comes from purely feeling good. When I get tickled like that, my laugh isn't exactly quiet either.

We were passing one of those canvas cantinas that had sprung up since Company F's arrival, and just then a knot of unshaven, red-eyed, slack-jawed drunks fell through the door flap and out into the street. They reminded me of a squirming pile of maggots tumbling all over each other, except these maggots were halfway dressed as United States soldiers.

The one who landed uppermost in the heap squinted up at me and said, "What are you laughin' at, you dirty Injun?"

Now I never was one to get riled easy, especially not on account of some drunk's slurred comment. As my Cherokee father used to say, "You can win a dispute with a skunk, but in the end you will smell like him."

So I just leaned over out of my saddle and real

15

gentle like said, " 'Pears to me you fellas already got all the trouble you need. I'm just passing by."

I was fixing to let it go at that when a big, red-haired lunk with a sunburned face got up from the pile. He looked at Simona heading on down the road and then he said to me, "What's that perty woman doin' with somebody as ugly as you? Hey, señoreeter," he called "come on back and get to know a real man."

Sometimes even a skunk puts his nose where it doesn't belong. Then it doesn't do any good ignoring him and hoping he'll go away; best to run him off at once. I wheeled Shawnee around and put her into a parade canter, a slow gallop, with her legs churning hard.

I headed right into that heap of blue-jacket maggots. Shawnee knocked one over with her shoulder while stomping on another. I kicked the third one out of the way and sent him sprawling over a guy rope. "Now lay there and listen," I advised them. "Señora Simona, that's missus to you, is a nice lady. Drunk or sober, you'd best not be insulting her where I can hear it." As I spoke, I dropped my hand to the coil of rawhide whip looped around my saddle horn.

That was when I first laid eyes on Jack Powers. The tent flap was flung back and a spruce-looking uniformed man with a big nose and a fleshy face stepped out. In one hand he held some cards. In the other fist was a Paterson Colt, and its .36-caliber barrel was pointed right at my breastbone. "Hold it right there," he ordered.

16

"Ease up a mite, Sergeant," I said. "I didn't really hurt your boys any. I was just teaching them some California manners."

"Get down off that horse," Powers ordered with a sneer. "You're under arrest for assaulting soldiers of the United States Army." To his men he added, "Pat, Ed, get up from there." Then he repeated his order to me to get down.

I turned Shawnee so as to step down with my back to those men. I will tell you plain, my spine half-expected a lead slug any second, but I needed to hide my whip hand as I shook out the lash.

"C'mon, hurry it up," I heard one of the drunks growl. He grabbed hold of one of my buckskin leggings. That's how I knew when to turn, because with that red-haired soldier right between me and Powers, the sergeant wouldn't dare shoot.

A sudden flick of the whip got Powers around the wrist of the hand gripping the gun. The Paterson discharged up into the air and then flew over into a patch of weeds.

I reversed my grip and drove the twelve-inch hickory wood handle into the forehead of the red-haired fellow and he dropped like a stone.

Shawnee was dancing and kicking up the dust, and when the other two soldiers tried to close with me, she cut one of them off. It was too tight a space for lash work now, so I stabbed the drunk named Ed in the gut with the hickory handle. His breath went out, and as he doubled over I hooked my left fist into the point of his chin. The shoulder that had caught the lance tip in the last battle of

17

the war with Mexico didn't like that and let me know it, but the blow served its purpose.

The third soldier circled out of range of Shawnee's hooves and tried to come at me with a knife. I needed to hurry. I could see Powers cussing and scrabbling in the dust, trying to recover the revolver from where it had landed in a mess of prickly pear cactus.

It's amazing how much force you can put into a twelve-inch piece of hickory if you've a mind to. I smashed one blow over the soldier's knife grip, then backhanded the man across the nose.

Powers was coming up with the pistol, so it was needful to turn my attention back to him. This time I let the popper on the bullwhip do my talking for me. The thin strip of knotted buckskin crossed Powers' cheek, splitting the flesh in a welt that stopped just short of his right eye.

The sergeant threw up his hand to his cheek, and the gun dropped again in the dirt. "Leave it there," I said, "or next time I won't spare your sight."

"Señor Andrew!" called Simona as she rattled back up to the scene. Only this time she had Colonel Stevenson with her.

"Sergeant!" ordered the colonel. "Bring your men to attention at once!"

"Colonel, this man . . ." Powers started in, but it was obvious his words didn't carry any weight with his commander.

"Forget it, Sergeant. The señora has already told me about the drunken insults. Besides, do you

18

know who this man is? Andrew Jackson Sinnickson has scouted for Colonel Fremont alongside of Kit Carson. Sergeant, those three men are on report, and put your own name down as well. Now, make your apologies."

There was some grumbling, but no open argument from the three soldiers or their sergeant. A few muttered words passed for apologies, and that seemed to satisfy the colonel.

But when I was coiling up the whip and got over next to Powers, this is what he said, "You may be holding all the cards right now, but there'll be other hands dealt."

CHAPTER 2

Fifteen months later I had all but forgot about Jack Powers and his threat. I had my own cattle spread all right, but things had not exactly worked out according to my calculations.

I was running a herd of about two hundred head, mostly rangy old rust-colored steers. They looked like the hide was stretched over their bones without any meat in between. I had picked up the land on the west side of California's Great Valley by settling an old ranchero's debt to a Yankee money lender.

I called my place Rancho Libre, or Freedom Ranch, figuring to honor both my American side and the Spanish speakers. Freedom grew well enough in the sage and creosote bush-covered hills, but precious little else did. Fact is, I should have named the spread Rancho Liebre, which sounds almost the same but means Rabbit Ranch. The only critters that thrived and grew to remarkable size were the jackrabbits.

To make matters worse, the hide business slumped. There was still no market for the meat, and after twenty years as dependable as the sunrise, hides were selling for less than two dollars apiece.

The solitude of the place gave me lots of time to think on what my future might hold. For companionship I had only the rabbits and a half-breed boy named Joaquin, whom I won in a card game. I didn't really own him, you understand, but he was only twelve and had nowhere else to go, and anyway, that's a tale for another time.

I also had a dog. At least I think he was *part* dog. Mostly he looked coyote by the set of his muzzle and the prick of his ears. He had a brush wolf's coat and tail, but with some added spots of tan mixed amongst the gray. He was thicker of body and short of limb too. Anyway, however careless of his parentage he might have been, he had adopted me. He trotted up to my campfire one night without so much as a by-your-leave, waited politely for supper, and stayed ever since.

Joaquin and I had built a brush hut with a canvas roof. It was to keep thieving critters away from our meager supplies. It did give us a place to sleep out of the rain, but April to October we slept out-of-doors.

The winter of my spell at Rancho Libre had been one of too little rain. The feed for the cows was thin, and all summer we had to keep moving them from one little canyon to the next.

We had a big fire blazing at the head of the draw, and after a supper of roasted rabbit, Joaquin had already drifted off to sleep. We took turn-about keeping watch. The few calves we had we could scarce afford to lose to the coyotes or the occasional bear or cougar down from the high country.

I was nodding myself, so I got up to throw another stick of mesquite on the fire. All at once Dog sat up and looked out over the dark valley. Then I heard it too — the clinking sound of stones struck by shod hooves. It came from the direction of the Tejon, or what they call the Badger Pass.

I shook Joaquin awake, gesturing for him to remain quiet. Boy and Dog faded back into the shadows away from the fire's glare.

My whip was coiled and hanging from my belt. I took my Allen over-and-under and moved silently on moccasined feet down the draw toward the herd.

As yet the cattle had made no stir. I passed quickly to the mouth of the draw and hunkered down to wait. The night was a dark one, with no moon, yet the sky was blazing with the light of millions of stars.

Now we had nothing worth stealing, and so little to fear from any robber. Still, only men in trouble or in a big hurry travel on moonless nights. This traveler, whoever he was, seemed headed straight for our camp.

A man's night vision is not as good as many of the Lord's creatures have, but his hearing can be a powerful tool if he's trained to use it. My Cherokee father had taught me to tell the shuffling run of the raccoon from the quick patter of the fox. I knew all the sounds the animals make going about their nightly routines.

Shawnee, my paint mare, who was grazing nearby, confirmed my thoughts about the intruder by lifting her head and snorting softly. The solitary rider was coming in cautiously from the east. He had dismounted and was leading his horse, and Shawnee stared at a dark clump of brush that had grown broader in the past minute.

Speaking might draw a bullet if mischief was meant, so I waited to see what was up. Presently there came a chuckle out of the darkness, and a gravelly voice said, "I swear, Andrew, you are as keen as ever, but you still got that dang piebald pony. Her white patches stand out like lanterns."

"Tor Fowler," I said. "What cause have you got for sneaking up thisaway?"

"I wasn't for certain it was you," he grumbled. "There's folks in this country now that that'll take a friendly howdy and answer back with buckshot."

"Come to the fire," I said, and he needed no further urging.

He seized on some leftover rabbit like he'd been without food for a week and devoted himself entirely to the business of eating. Joaquin came back into the light and stared in wide-eyed wonder at this apparition.

Tor Fowler was a mountain man and a wanderer. He still sported the fringed buckskins of one who was more at home with the solitude of the great peaks than the company of men. He had come west as a scout for Fremont. Fowler and I had been together in the days of the War with Mexico. At its conclusion, when I saw the chance to settle down and build something, he saw creeping civil-

23

ization and felt the urge to drift back into the mountains.

When he had filled himself moderately full, he sat back and wiped his pointed chin on the sleeve of his jacket. His eyes above the sharp beak of his nose twinkled back into mine and gave the lie to the otherwise hardness of his features.

"Guess you wonder what brung me?" he said at last.

"I figured you'd tell me when you were ready," I acknowledged. " 'Seek to know another's business and you'll always learn more than you care to,' Pastor Metcalfe used to say."

Fowler nodded sagely. "True enough, but what I've got to say is like to be everybody's business afore long. Have you heard tell of the gold strike up Coloma way?"

"Gold strike?" I could feel my eyebrows raise clear up to the top of my forehead. "Fowler, you are about the last man on earth I'd expect to believe in fairy tales."

"Knew you'd say that," Fowler replied, unruffled. "Try this on for size: Do you remember that Sutter fella that kept all them Injuns like slaves to work his wheat fields?"

"Sure. Styled himself captain. Even dressed up a hundred scrawny Nishinam in moth-eaten Russian army uniforms. Called them his soldiers."

"The very same," Fowler agreed, with a sidelong glance at me. "Well, all them Injuns have dropped their hoes and their fancy green coats and skedaddled."

24

"All of them?"

"Ever' one. Sutter's screamin' and nobody pays him any mind. Why, even some Germans he hired to build his mills just up and tossed away their hammers and saws to grab up picks and shovels."

I considered the words Fowler spoke. This wasn't the first time people had expected to find mineral wealth in the Sierras. Way back in Old Spanish days, three hundred years before, California was reputed to be a land so rich that even the tools and weapons were made of gold. 'Course, the same stories told of how Queen Calafia ruled over a kingdom inhabited only by women! "Fowler," I said, talking politely, "Don Will Reed told me how, in '41 or '42, some vaquero pulled up a handful of wild onions and found gold dust in amongst the roots. Don Will said it was true, but the little pocket played out and never amounted to much."

A crafty grin stole across Fowler's face. With his pointed features it gave him a strong resemblance to a fox. He'd probably have approved of the comparison, but I held it back just the same.

As the boy and I watched, Fowler reached inside his buckskin jacket. Lifting a small doe-hide pouch that hung around his neck, he pulled it over his head and hefted its weight. "Come on over here, son," he said to Joaquin. He passed the leather sack to the boy and gestured for Joaquin to shake it into his hand. We all scooted up next to the firelight to see. Even Dog crowded in, his ears all pricked up and his head cocked to one side.

25

Joaquin pried the knotted strings apart and up-ended the pouch. Into his palm dropped not one, but a dozen dull gleaming lumps. The smallest was the size of a pea, while the biggest approached the dimensions of the last joint of Fowler's brown, scarred thumb.

"Dug 'em out of a place no bigger than this," Fowler said, using his wiry arms to show a space the size of a washtub.

"Is it really oro, señor? Really gold?" asked Joaquin. The boy's voice trembled a little.

"Tested and proved," Fowler vowed. "That big rascal is worth close to thirty dollars all by hisself. Altogether you're holdin' maybe a hundred fifty, two hundred dollars' worth."

"All right, Joaquin, enough gawking," I said sternly. "You and Dog make a circle of the herd and then come back for some shut-eye."

"But Señor Andrew," Joaquin started to protest.

"No arguments. Get going." The boy handed the shiny pebbles back with some reluctance, I thought.

When Joaquin was out of earshot, I asked Fowler why he had come so far to bring me this news. "You must have ridden three hundred miles to tell me about your good fortune," I said. "Why?"

Fowler looked over his shoulder at the gloomy dark of the hillside before replying. "I'll tell you straight out," he said at last. "These here nuggets does strange things to folks." He searched my face as if reading trail signs. "It won't pay a man to work alone in them wild canyons — but it surely

26

would be worse for him to be amongst partners he couldn't rely on."

I nodded my agreement with this assessment and encouraged him to go on. "Well, sir, there's nought but four men in this old world I'd trust to partner up with where gold is concerned. Two of them is off somewheres in the high lonesome, and the other two is you and Will Reed."

Having the approval of a man like Tor Fowler is akin to the honor of having the President hang a medal around your neck. Or rather, it's like being complimented on the keenness of your eyesight by an eagle.

"Thanks," I said, "but are things truly so lawless?"

"Not so far," he admitted. "The finding is still easy but the elbow room only so-so. And greed can't be made to hold still. Before I came south there was already folks from Monterrey and Frisco comin' up to stake claims. And I seen two bunches square off over a promising hunk of creek bed."

"Anybody killed?"

"Not for want of tryin'. When the score was five to two of folks still standin', the losers moved downstream a ways."

"I've got my ranching to think of," I protested. "I can't just turn my herd loose."

Fowler looked amused, but he had the good grace to hide it. I'm certain that the same image of the rangy cows flashed through his mind as was etched in my own. "I'd not expect you to leave your herd," he said, tugging at a shaggy forelock.

"I come here first to sound you out afore ridin' on to Santa Barbara to see Will Reed. You are interested, ain'tcha?"

I started to argue, but my heart wasn't in it. Ranching was not exactly turning out like I expected. "Let me have another look at your poke," I requested.

A grin crept over Tor Fowler's lean features. "I'll do better than that," he said. "I'll leave half of it here with you . . . partner."

Fowler rolled up next to the fire and slept. Joaquin and I took turn-about on guard, and when I came back at gray dawn from my last watch, Fowler was already up and gone.

It didn't surprise me any that he had not said goodbye. Mountain men were always wisps of smoke in their ways of coming and going. Not sleeping past dawn nor announcing a departure were two hard-learned lessons of survival that I'll not begrudge a man.

Joaquin seemed to think he might have dreamed the whole thing. I saw him wake and rub his eyes; then as the recollection struck him, he looked around for Fowler. Stretching his hands out toward the smoldering fire, he turned one palm upward as he remembered the nuggets. "Señor," he asked me, "was your amigo, Señor Fowler, was he really here last night?"

I unbuttoned a flap pocket of my flannel shirt and passed over one of the golden lumps left me by my new partner.

CHAPTER 3

It took Tor Fowler only three days to ride to Santa Barbara and back. When he returned, he was accompanied by a pair of Don Will Reed's vaqueros and a loaded pack mule.

"Hello the camp," Fowler hollered, riding up in broad daylight. "Where's that Sinnickson feller who's about to be a rich man?"

Fowler explained that Will Reed, while fascinated with the gold and plainly itching to go for the adventure of it, could not leave home. "Seems that the Señora Francesca is in a delicate condition," Fowler said, "and Will don't think it right to leave her."

"And you," I said to the vaqueros. "Did he send you to go in his place?"

"No, Señor Andrew," responded the one named Rodrigo. "Don Will sent us to drive your cattle to his San Marcos range. He says to tell you we will keep them safe against your return."

"Right neighborly of Don Will too," commented Fowler. "Said for us to take right off. Even sent us some supplies." He indicated the mule.

"Seems everything's settled then, with one exception," I said. "Joaquin, I want you to go with the herd and stay with the Reed family until I return."

"Oh no, señor!" protested Joaquin with alarm. "You and I are compadres, partners, you said, just like you and Señor Fowler are partners. You must not leave me behind!"

"Now, Joaquin," I began, trying to reason with the boy. "This won't be a pleasure trip. Things may get rough. Best you remain —"

"No, Señor Andrew," he said firmly. "If you make me go to the Reed rancho, I will run away to come and look for you."

I looked to Fowler for help, but he just shrugged. "Puts me in mind of me and you, Andrew," he said. "Guess he don't leave us no choice but to take him along."

We traveled north for three days, skirting the western edge of the swampy lands and following the course of the San Joaquin River. The morning of the fourth day found us across the stream bed from a tent settlement by the name of Tuleburg. Apt name too for a place that only rose above the cattails to the height of a canvas-covered ridge-pole. It was near the junction of the San Joaquin and the Calaveras and looked more like a haphazardly laid-out army post than a town.

But humans being what they are, everybody tries to invest his efforts, no matter how modest, with a little grandeur. (Like me and my big plans for Rancho Libre, I reckon.) Anyway, this miserable collection of motley gray awnings and shacks was already styling itself a city. There was even a move afoot to rename the place for Commodore Stockton of Bear Flag War fame.

Fowler braced a merchant to inquire if anyone had asked Stockton for his permission, but the shopkeeper did not see the humor in it.

We were of a mind to push on to the location of Fowler's find on the south fork of the American, but talk around Tuleburg stopped us.

"Whereabouts you gents figure to make your pile?" inquired a fat man selling two-bit shovels for ten dollars apiece.

"Up Coloma way," said Fowler vaguely.

"A pity," commented the chubby hardware salesman with a shake of his head that made his jowls quiver.

"Why? What's wrong with it?" I demanded.

"Nothing. Nothing at all, 'cept it's altogether overrun with folks. Shiploads of whalers, army deserters, scads of foreigners from outlandish places like Peru . . . even kanakas from the cannibal islands. You won't find room enough to swing a cat. No sir, none atall."

"So? Why tell us? You got a better idea?"

"Just thought you might want to turn up the Calaveras. Some mighty fine big strikes up yonder. Yessir, brand new."

"So's you can sit downstream here and sell ever'body their supplies? No thank you," Fowler said. "We don't need your advice."

"Ease up, Fowler," I suggested. Then to the merchant I inquired, "This new strike got a name?"

"Angel's Camp," was the reply.

After we had passed on out of earshot I turned to Fowler. "What do you think really?" I asked him. "Do we go on or turn up the creek here?"

"I just don't like ever'body knowin' my business," he said. "Sutter's land was gettin' awful overrun. Let's go see what Angel's Camp has to offer for a couple old sinners like us."

The trail we followed up into the Calaveras country had plainly been hacked out of the wilderness not long before. The path was not yet passable to wagons or wheeled carts of any kind. In fact, it was scarcely wide enough for two loaded mules to pass each other. Portions of the way wound through hewn-down clumps of elderberry bushes. The debris of the discarded branches, heavy with fruit, still littered the ground.

Fowler pointed out the wasted and rotting piles of dark red berries. "Shameful," he said. "Injuns hereabouts make their winter stores up outta poundin' acorn meal and bear fat together with elderberry juice. Keeps right well too."

Ahead of us as we rode, another traveler bound for the mines came into view. He was a smallish man, dressed respectably in a black suit. He was leading a loaded mule, while he himself rode "shank's mare."

The path just before us crested a knob of bare rock, then made a sharp turn away from the edge of a sheer dropoff. The stream bed lay about eighty feet below, and another eighty feet or so of hillside hung above us.

The lone prospector was struggling with his dark-coated Mexican mule. It had chosen the exact worst place, as mules and humans often do, to turn balky.

"Come on now," the man demanded in a clipped and nasally voice. He dug in his heels and pulled on the lead rope as he backed up the hill. The mule responded in kind, squatting on its haunches and bracing its forelegs against the stone face of the cliff.

Fowler, who was riding in the lead of our threesome, called a halt. As I have said, the trail was too narrow for us to get around the obstruction, so all we could do was keep out of the way of the battle.

We had dismounted and were watching the struggle with some amusement when from behind us I heard the low "hoo, hoo, hoo" of a horned owl. It must have registered with Fowler at the same instant as me, because he whipped his Hawken out of its beaded scabbard just as I pivoted the Allen up and cocked both hammers.

You see, as my Cherokee daddy taught me, when a nightbird calls in daylight, it's time to wake up! A low rumble and a pattering sound, like a light rain, sounded from above us on the cliff. It gained rapidly in volume and intensity as the tumble became a roar. "Rock slide," I yelled, slapping Shawnee on the rump to get her moving and hollering for Joaquin to get down. With an enemy behind us, there was nothing to do but hug the ground and pray.

All three of our horses and our pack mule went clattering back down the trail. A boulder the size of my head came bounding down the hillside. It was aiming straight for Joaquin when I grabbed him by the arm and rolled over and over with him to get out of the block's path.

Not six feet from us the rock struck something and gave an immense leap into the air, like someone who just sat on a bee. The stone careened overhead in a high arc and flew off into the canyon. After that first flying headache, the hillside seemed alive with bouncing rocks.

A yell erupted from the throat of the stranger. His panicked mule swung around violently and swept the man about like a game of crack-the-whip.

It was an act of providence that saved the man's life. His grip broke free of the lead rope that he'd been tugging on, and the sudden motion flung him aside some distance away from the mule.

Not five seconds later, the main force of the avalanche swept right over where he had been standing. The mule gave a high-pitched scream of terror and was carried over the precipice in the blink of an eye.

All this happened in less time than it takes to tell. The roar of the slide had changed back to the pattering of odd stones and loose gravel before the body of the unfortunate mule had scarce hit bottom. Fowler and I were already sighting over our rifles in expectation of the attack that would follow this ambush.

There was a movement near the top of the hill, and Fowler and I fired almost in the same heartbeat. It was too far to make out plain, but a swarthy-complected figure in a buckskin shirt cried out, then turned and ran up over the hill and out of sight.

"Stay with Fowler!" I yelled to Joaquin, and I took off after our horses and all our belongings. You may wonder how I could charge off that way, since there was no way of knowing how many enemies were waiting for me and without having had a chance to reload. The answer is simple: I was so hopping mad, I didn't stop to think about it! Anyway, I still had the shotgun barrel of the Allen primed and ready. I was not about to let any cowardly murderous thieves succeed in getting away with our possessions if I could prevent it.

I ran along, zigging and zagging down the slope, hoping to take the thieves unawares by appearing from an unexpected direction. I knew Shawnee would not have run far, and I hoped that the other animals would take their cues from her and stop when she did.

The next level spot I came to was a clearing ringed by oaks and elderberry bushes. In the center of the circle of brush were our three horses. They were milling around, stamping and snorting like steam engines. But there was no trace of the pack mule and all our supplies.

I debated with myself over mounting up and riding after the robbers, but the hot anger was off me by then, replaced by more temperate reasoning. I wouldn't gain much by spurring after them alone, not when Fowler and I could follow them plain enough after he was mounted again.

About this time, Dog came trotting up with a scrap of buckskin clenched between his teeth. He dropped his trophy at my feet and wagged. "You did good," I praised him. "Here I was wondering where you'd got off to, and you were on the job all the time."

I picked up the fragment of leather and the lead ropes of the three horses and started back up the trail. Halfway to the rockslide I met Fowler headed down. "You all right?" he asked.

"Only half," I admitted. "They got away with the mule, but Dog here gave them something to remember us by. Where's Joaquin?"

"Left him with Ames. That's the feller that almost took a swan dive with *his* mule. Yankee from the sound of him. Piece of rock grazed him across the head, an' he's lucky he ain't kilt. Joaquin's patchin' him up. We can send them along to camp while we get on the trail of those bushwhackers."

The rest of the way back, Fowler and I discussed the attack. "Injuns, you figger?" Fowler asked, squinting at the shredded fabric.

"Hard to say. By his coloring, dark like mine, the one who caused the slide might have been Indian, but he could have been Mexican or Spaniard. He lit a shuck too quick for me to get a good look. I never saw any others. Dog left his regards on one, but this piece of buckskin could have come from you just as easy as an Indian."

36

"Anybody mad enough at you to want to kill you?"

I laughed. "Not so far as I know. How about you?"

Fowler gave the matter serious reflection. "Some folks I know ain't gonna go outta their way to shake my hand or buy me a seegar, but I don't recollect anyone after my scalp personal like."

When we came up to the slide, Joaquin was tying off the knot on a strip of shirttail that he had wound around the bleeding man's head. The slightly built figure in black was seated on the ground gritting his teeth. One side of his head was swelled up in one place the size of an apple, and the man's complexion was gray as the rock dust.

The man stuck out his hand. "I'm obliged to you and this boy," he said in a Yankeefied voice. With evident difficulty he struggled to his feet. "Ee-yup. Best get on with rounding up my —" Ames swayed and would have pitched over on his face if Tor and I had not caught him.

"Guess that settles what we do next," Fowler said with a shrug as he tossed the unconscious Mr. Ames across his shoulder. "We'd best take this one and Joaquin on to Angel's Camp, an' then we'll get to trackin'."

CHAPTER 4

I think it safe to record that our entry into any town or village back in the States would have occasioned quite a stir. Consider our appearance: A mixed-breed boy and a brown and weathered buckskin-clad trapper, leading a horse with an unconscious man tied onto the saddle. These were followed by a down-at-the-heels rancher riding on an Indian pony, with a half-grown wolf pup ranging alongside.

And yet, for California in 1848, not only did our assemblage not cause any commotion, we did not even provoke any comments! Anyone who had ridden into Angel's Camp that autumn afternoon would have recognized the reason at once. Nothing in our dress, manner, or composition would have been the least out of the ordinary. Fact is, while no one paid us any heed, we all found ourselves staring around quite a bit.

A pretty little valley, ringed by low hills, lay before us. The nearer slopes were studded with gnarled oaks and gooseberry patches, while the farther wore manzanita thickets and tall, shapely pines. The center of our view was a bare plain where two creeks converged, or rather, what would have been a bare plain if it had not been covered with tents and canvas awnings, rude huts, and brush lean-tos. And the architects of those human habitations — now there was a sight!

A split plank footbridge crossed the larger channel of the two creeks, and over this rustic roadway passed a parade to equal the sideshow of any circus. Three men, lately of some infantry regiment as demonstrated by the remains of their tattered uniforms, were likewise marked as deserters by the lack of any company insignia.

Waiting for the ex-soldiers to pass was a short man whose knees were escaping through the rents in his trousers even as his curly black hair escaped from under the odd bonnet-shaped hat he wore. A plain tan vest was an ill match for his overly large gray-striped frock coat.

Behind this fashionable Californian were two tall men in long serapes that reached to their knees. Flat-crowned, broad-brimmed hats and a haughty and aristocratic manner made me guess that their homeland was the Argentine.

And what did these assorted specimens of God's infinite wit have in common? They were all miners; true examples of the strange breed known as prospectors. Between the six there were five shovels, three picks, four tin pans, and a determined air of invincible good fortune. What's more, these six were just the sample on display, so to speak. In the creek bed and on the hillsides all around, there were a hundred more, swinging their picks and swirling the pans.

But we had no time to reflect on these impressions. There was the injured Mr. Ames to be seen to and the not inconsequential matter of our stolen property.

We directed our course toward the most imposing structure visible. This was, I regret to say, nothing more than a long, low tent covered in stained gray sailcloth. Three sides were sheltered by the canvas awning, but the fourth was open to the elements.

When we got closer, we could see that our target was in fact some sort of public building, since a stream of miners were coming and going from the premises. "Hello the tent," Fowler called out.

"Store, if you please, or trading post," retorted the man who responded to Fowler's salutation. "Either sounds more dignified than 'tent.' "

"That's as may be," Fowler returned, "but I'm seeking a doctor or what passes for one around here, and if I can't find him in this tent, then it don't matter what you call it!"

"Easy, friend," said the portly proprietor through teeth clamped around a short-stemmed pipe. "I didn't see you had wounded. Bring him in; this is as civilized as it gets." Then to the interior of the tent he shouted, "Patrick, clean off that counter — we got an injured man here!"

Now I like to think that I don't surprise easy, and I try my dead level best not to show consternation even when I feel it, but the identity of that storekeeper's assistant surely did give me pause. You see, it was Patrick Dunn, one of those New York soldier fellows with whom I'd clashed

40

back in Santa Barbara.

If he recognized me, he gave no sign of it. At the time, I thought that either he'd been too drunk during the brawl to remember me, or perhaps he'd just decided to let the past lay. Anyway, I figured if he was content to leave it alone, so should I.

Dunn busied himself moving a stack of flannel shirts and a crate of plug tobacco off the rough-hewn plank table. We stretched Ames out, and the store's owner examined the Yankee's head. Ames was still unconscious, but his color was better. He flinched and moaned some when the wound was unbandaged and cleaned, and it started to bleed again.

During the procedure, the man doing the doctoring introduced himself. "Name's Angel," he said. "Henry Angel. This is my store. Doc Den is over at Murphy's Diggings today seeing to a man that came near to cutting his thumb off, but I reckon I can stitch this fellow up. How'd this happen?"

As I filled him in on our experience with the rockslide and the robbery, I watched his face grow grim. "Thievin' Digger Indians," he said. "They just get bolder and bolder. Well, it's got to stop."

I tried to explain that the identity of the attackers was by no means certain and that Fowler and I could track them with the aid of Dog, but he seemed not to be listening. "Patrick," he ordered Dunn, "round up a half dozen of the boys and we'll go teach those savages a lesson."

Henry Angel and the other Angel's Campers had

41

it set in their minds that the local Miwok Indian tribe was behind the attack on our party. It was the miners' intention to see that retribution was carried out. In the words of a man named Cannon, a burly prospector who wore his long black beard tucked into the front of his red flannel shirt, "It was them thievin' Digger Injuns, I tell you! We oughta ride straight to their village and burn 'em out!"

Angel had Patrick Dunn remain behind to watch over his store. Privately, I thought this was setting the fox to guard the henhouse, but I kept my peace. As long as Dunn was acting the part of an upright citizen, there seemed to be no cause to butt in.

We rode out then, Angel and Fowler and me in the lead, followed by Cannon and the others. Ames, with his freshly stitched and bandaged scalp, was tucked into a cot. I left Joaquin and Dog with orders to watch over him.

We were within half a mile of the site of the ambush when Fowler called for a halt. He directed the miners to follow a trail that veered off down toward the creek. "What's up?" Angel wanted to know. "I thought you said they jumped you up on the main road."

"Did say that," replied Fowler tersely. "Reckoned you could go by where the mule belongin' to that Ames feller musta landed. See if you can salvage some of his things, whilst Andrew and me pick up the track up top."

I knew without being told that Fowler was trying to keep the miners from attacking the Indian camp.

Led by Cannon, the prospectors were of a mind to shoot first and raise questions after. Such an attitude isn't healthy for those on the receiving end. It would be the shank of the afternoon in one more hour. If Fowler's device worked, the Angel's Campers might spend long enough gathering up the scattered supplies that it would then be time to head back.

There were few noteworthy clues on the high ledge above the trail. We found where the swarthy-faced attacker had tied his mount while he prepared the ambush and where he had used a redwood limb to tip over the rock to start the slide. Beyond that we found nothing to identify the race of the man. "I don't know, Andrew," Tor Fowler said. "Does this strike you as Miwok doings? I've fought plenty of Injuns in my time, but I never saw anything as bald-faced as this."

I agreed with him. "They must have known that an ambush of white men this close to a mining camp would bring destruction down on their heads, double-quick. Even if they weren't expecting any of us to survive, who else is there around to blame?"

"That's the point, ain't it?" he mused. "No matter who done it, the Injuns'll catch the blame."

"All the more reason for us to track down the real culprits," I said.

We started to follow the trail that we were certain would lead back to the site of Dog's encounter with the robbers. We were no more than a hundred yards along the ridge when the peaceful afternoon was shattered by a sound like a herd of buffalo crashing through the brush of the creek bed. Wild whoops and the explosions of gunfire followed close behind.

"Come on!" Fowler shouted, spurring his bay. "Someone's catching it!"

Across the slide rock we flew, sparks bursting from Shawnee's shoes as we clattered slantwise down the slope. I was practically lying along Shawnee's backbone to keep my weight back on her skidding haunches. I had the reins out at arms' length, like steering by the tiller of a sailing ship, but the fact is, I was relying totally on her instincts to get us through.

We swung sharply to the left, narrowly avoiding a drop of a hundred feet or more. Shawnee's hooves somehow found a ledge that was no more than a crack in the rock face. In between jolting gasps for breath, I found myself wondering who it was we were risking our necks for, and if they would even appreciate it should we come to grief on their account before reaching the bottom.

A flurry of gunfire up the canyon a ways told us of the ongoing battle. A flock of doves burst out of their roost in the cottonwoods at what was then eye level for Fowler and me. "Hold on, Andrew!" he called over his shoulder as he and the bay plunged ahead. I could not see past the body of his horse to know what he was warning me about, and perhaps it was just as well. We had run out of hillside, and the last of our headlong charge carried us through a dozen feet of air.

Shawnee took the jump in fine shape, landing in deep sand with scarcely a break in her gallop. Wheeling around like a cavalry squad on parade, Fowler and I set off toward the screen of trees and brush that obscured our view of the fight. I shucked the scabbard of the Allen. Out of the corner of my eye I noted Fowler draw his rifle as well. As we got closer, we heard cries of fear and shouts of rage mingled with the explosions.

Our swoop toward the conflict was cut short by a small dark-haired figure in buckskin and faded flannel that burst from the willows right under my nose. I saw an ax waving in the air, but as I brought the Allen to bear, Shawnee reared and spoiled my aim. The menacing figure jogged aside, making me hurry my sights. I had just drawn a bead again when Fowler's cry stopped me. "Don't shoot, Andrew," he yelled. "It's a woman!"

And so it proved. The slight form that scampered off into the brush and out of sight had a reedwork basket strapped to her back. Over the rim of the hamper, an infant-sized fist could be seen waving defiantly.

I grinned weakly and waved my thanks at Fowler. I wanted to think that even without his warning, my own senses would have prevented a mishap, but then I remembered that Shawnee's unexpected motion had also been needed to keep me from firing. I breathed a prayer of thanks, but the nearness of the tragedy made my stomach churn.

We charged on into the battle, fearful of what

we would find, and found that the reality was worse than we feared. An unearthly keening had joined the other noises. It was a high-pitched wail that began at the level of a wolf's howl and went straight up to the screech of a red-tailed hawk.

The portion of the creek bottom toward which we rode was an island at a wetter season of year. At the time of which I write, it was a low knoll of cottonwoods and willows surrounded by a rocky plain through which ran a thin trickle of water. The hillock was ringed by Angel's Campers with their rifles cocked and steady on a small knot of Indians that had retreated to the clump of trees.

I've lived with Indians and I've fought Indians, but I never before saw anything so one-sided dignified with the word battle. A wounded Miwok man sat on the ground, hugging a bullet-shattered forearm and rocking softly with the pain. Another dead man was draped over a boulder. There were three bullet holes in his back. In his back!

The shrieking sound was coming from the throat of a Miwok woman who was huddled her the limp body of a small boy. A young Miwok woman and two children stood looking on, their eyes wide with fright.

At the moment we rode up, Cannon was saying, "What are we waiting for? I say we shoot 'em down and put a stop to their thievin' *and* that caterwaulin', the filthy savages." Without waiting for any agreement on the part of the others, he raised his Hall carbine to his shoulder.

Fowler never paused in the headlong rush of

the bay. Without drawing rein the least bit, his gelding barrelled into Cannon's mount. It was a classic *golpe de caballo,* the strike with the horse, that would have done credit to one of Will Reed's vaqueros.

Cannon's arms went straight up and the rifle flew from his hands, the shot exploding into the air as it went. The black-bearded miner followed the carbine in flight, landing heavily on the river-rounded stones with a cry of pain.

A friend of Cannon's made to swing his revolver around to bear on Fowler, but I was ready for him. My lash flicked out and around his wrist, and soon after he joined his partner on the canyon's rocky floor.

"You'd both best lie there awhile," Fowler ordered, swinging his rifle around the group.

"And if the rest of you don't want to join them," I added, "you'd better keep real still."

"What is this?" Henry Angel said. "I don't get it. We come out here to catch the snakes that attacked you boys. We nab them red-handed lootin' Ames's supplies, and now you stick up for them. It don't make sense!"

"How do you know that this particular bunch of Indians ambushed us?" I asked.

"Just look!" spouted Cannon from his place on the ground. He abandoned caution in favor of rage. "They got their hands full of mining gear!"

The squaw who was standing dropped a tin pan as if it had turned blazing hot in her grasp. It clattered and banged on the rocks, but brought the wailing to a sudden stop. The woman with the dead child continued moaning, but softly.

I said, "You understand English? You speak it?"

"I speak," replied the woman who dropped the pan. "We find dead mule and no man around. We no kill."

"Pack of lyin' rats," Cannon announced.

"Friend," Fowler said, "I ain't gonna warn you again not to interrupt," and Cannon subsided.

"We no kill," the squaw repeated. "We find only."

"Where were you coming from before you found this?"

The woman gestured downstream. "We pick berries. Fill baskets. Go home."

I pointed toward a reed-carrying basket and motioned for her to upend it. As she obliged, several gallons of dark red berries spilled across the creek bed, blending into the dark red blood of the dead man.

"All right," Angel observed, "but that doesn't prove anything. They could still have caused the rockslide when they saw a way to get something more valuable than berries." Several of the miners nodded their agreement, especially Cannon.

I ignored this and continued to question the woman. "Did you see anything on your way here?" I asked. "Meet anyone?"

She thought for a minute, then said, "Two men. A mule, going toward valley."

"Indian?"

She shook her head no. "One Spanish, one white."

"So what?" Ames said. "You don't know that those two, if they really existed, had your animal. Loaded pack mules are all over these hills."

"Think hard," I urged the woman. "Did anything seem wrong with those two men?"

She looked puzzled at the question; then a light of comprehension widened her eyes. "White man's britches," she said. "Seat torn out."

I reached inside my shirt then. Retrieving the scrap of buckskin brought me by Dog, I held it aloft for all to see. One by one, the miners looked from the leather fragment to the woman holding her dead son. Cannon's friend hastily mounted up, and the five turned their mounts around and started up the trail toward home, leaving Angel and Cannon with Fowler and me and the Miwoks. Fowler gestured with his rifle for Cannon to pick himself up and get on his horse.

Fowler looked as stern as only a mountain man that was part grizzly bear could look. He stared pointedly at Cannon and Angel, then turned to study the Miwok man who was struggling to stand and the mother gathering up the body of her child. Angel did not miss the suggestion in Fowler's look. "We can help you to your camp," he said.

"No!" said the younger woman fiercely, gesturing with her fist at Cannon. "You not touch them!"

We four white men turned our horses then, riding away from that place of grief and cruel injustice. Fowler urged his bay up between Cannon and Angel. "Seems those 'savages,' as you call them, got a sight more dignity than you," Fowler observed. "She spit in your eye, didn't she?"

Cannon hawked and spat noisily. "Lousy vermin. Still shoulda kilt 'em. Teach the rest a lesson."

Fowler never looked over or gave any sign. He just unloaded a backhanded blow against Cannon's temple with a fist like a smith's hammer. The bearded man was again swept from his saddle, this time landing on his head. He looked around stupidly as his horse ran off toward camp. "Thought you'd say that," Fowler observed as we rode on.

Tor and I left Henry Angel behind to fetch Cannon's mount. Far up the trail we did not speak, yet I knew we were of like minds. Calaveras Canyon, which the old Spaniards had called *Skulls*, had certainly lived up to its grim name. The site of an ancient Indian battle, this place had been littered with human bones left to bleach in the sun. Like Calvary of old, Calaveras had become the scene of a new crucifixion. A man and a child had been murdered, and the white man's law offered no punishment for the crime. To butcher a Miwok Indian for sport or target practice was no worse than shooting a bear. To kill an Indian suspected of thieving was considered a white man's duty!

" 'Twas almost Eden when I first come here," Tor muttered at last. "If we live a while, Andrew, there won't be no more Injuns left for swine like Cannon to kill."

50

I nodded and followed Tor as he spurred his mount up the embankment and off the trail into the cover of the woods. Although we did not speak of it aloud, we felt the nearness of evil at our backs.

CHAPTER 5

There were more remarks made in Angel's Camp of white men sticking up for the despised Digger Injuns than of the fact that two innocent people had been killed and another seriously hurt. If Fowler and I were not exactly shunned, nobody was overanxious for our company, either.

That suited us just fine. Ames was awake and feeling as well as could be expected for a man who had come within an inch of having his head split open like a ripe melon.

But they don't call Yankees "hardheaded" for nothing. Ames was up and around after only one day. He said that the inside of his skull was buzzing louder than his family's cloth mill back home. "Reckon you saved my life," he managed to remark to Fowler and me. "Ee-yup. I'm mighty grateful."

When Ames heard that our supplies had been stolen in the same attack made on him, he insisted that we share equally in his recovered provisions. We found ourselves outfitted once again, as good as before.

Ames was a trader in dry goods. He had been in the Kingdom of Hawaii for several years, operating an outpost of his family's business, when he heard about the California gold.

With typical Yankee shrewdness, Ames had recognized at once that the miners would only bring a limited amount of supplies with them. They would need to replace boots, clothing, and equipment, and they would want it from the nearest source they could find.

"You won't find me breaking my back, no sir," he said. "You boys will be bringing gold straight to me without me digging a lick."

Ames had come alone to the diggings with only a single mule load of supplies in order to get the lay of the land. He had a ship full of goods waiting in San Francisco for his word to freight them up into the hills.

"I'll snoop around here for a few days and look into the competition," Ames said, meaning Henry Angel's store. "Then we'll see. I might move on up a ways."

The creek banks around Angel's Camp were humming with the activity of mining. Fowler and I had to travel a day's journey farther upstream to locate a likely stretch of as yet unoccupied creek. We decided to commence prospecting there.

The first order of business was to stake our claim. At this time, the commonly agreed on rules for the Calaveras region allowed each miner to claim a space ten-feet square. We marked the corners of three adjoining squares, one each for Fowler and me and a third for Joaquin, by writing our names on scraps of paper nailed to posts along the stream bank. In appearance our claim was then a thirty-foot rectangle that extended ten feet in width up from the water's southern edge.

My claim, which was the farthest upstream, commenced just at the middle of a sharp bend in the stream. We had agreed for each man to examine the prospects of his own claim first; then we would concentrate on whichever square showed the most promise.

I filled my first pan with dirt from the bank and carried it to the icy water. Squatting down beside the creek, I swirled the water around and around, washing the mud and the lighter gravel over the side. When this had been done until only the heaviest material remained, I tilted the pan toward the sunlight and poked around in it with my forefinger.

"No chispa," muttered a disappointed Joaquin, looking over my shoulder. "No spark."

"Don't be too sure," I said. From the iron particles that remained I separated a heavy flake of material. I scratched it with my knife and it did not shatter; between my teeth it felt soft and not gritty. "It's gold, right enough," I announced. "I heard tell that this Calaveras gold was real dark, almost black."

That panful of dirt contained twelve flecks or bits of gold — scarcely enough to cover my fingertip with a button-sized circle of the precious metal, but this was still a good prospect, since the real pocket was not to be expected on the surface.

It took two days to dig down to bedrock, saving

all the dirt that came out of that hole for later washing. When we hit a layer of quartz, we knew we had reached our limit.

Unlike Fowler's experience, there were no nuggets lying in the bottom of the ancient stream bed. We found a few pieces the size of kernels of wheat tucked into a crack in the quartz face, but nothing to get real excited about.

Resolving to see how the excavated dirt would pan out, we began to work through that chore next. We would then decide whether to continue working these claims or abandon them in favor of moving the search somewhere else.

Our first week of panning the heap of dirt brought us two ounces of the coarse, black flakes, or about thirty dollars' worth at the going rate. Not a fortune by any account, but not a bust either.

I reminded myself that I owned a herd of steers that I couldn't clear two dollars apiece for, if that, and five dollars for a day's work didn't seem half bad.

We didn't actually divide it up right then, of course. That gold went into the leather pouch that Tor Fowler still wore around his neck.

Panning is backbreaking, muscle-tearing, finger-numbing work. Hunkering down on your haunches for eight or ten hours with your feet slipping into a snow-melt stream is no Sunday social. Right off we saw that we needed to build a rocker.

Fowler felled a cedar tree and cut a round from it that we slabbed into passable planks. It wasn't that this was so altogether easy as it sounds — rather it was the anticipation that it would improve our gold-finding ability that made the work pass pleasantly.

A rocker looks for all the world like a baby's cradle, which is its other common name. The earth to be washed is loaded into a kind of hopper at the top. When water is poured over it, the gold-bearing dirt sifts through a crack down to a slanted board set with crossbars called riffles to catch the gold. The curved runners on which the thing sets and an upright handle allow the whole device — water, mud, gold, and all — to be rocked from side to side. It is the back and forth motion of the water that separates the gold from the soil.

Fowler fitted the last of the whittled cedar pegs into the holes cut to secure the handle, then stood back to admire our creation. "Whew, Andrew," he observed. "It's a good thing this ain't really for no baby. No child would want to be rocked in this contraption! Why, he'd up and die of shame afore he'd let hisself be humiliated thisaway!"

I will admit that it was a touch lopsided. "Let's see how she works," I said. "Even an ugly old buggy perks up when it has gold fittings."

Three men is just the right number to work a rocker. One hauls the pay dirt, one lifts the un-countable buckets of water required to run through it, and the third keeps the cradle in motion. Fowler and me took turnabout working the rocker and hauling the water. Joaquin loaded in a shovelful of dirt every so often and cleaned the gold dust off the riffles and into our poke, so his part wasn't too tough.

It isn't that the cradle makes the work so much easier, it's just that you can sift your way through so much more dirt in a day's time. We ended our first month in the diggings with three hundred dollars of gold dust, a working system for proceeding, and an all-fired hankering for something to eat besides bean and jerky stew.

"Warm tortillas," Joaquin daydreamed aloud. "Pollo con arroz, chicken and rice like Señora Simona fixes at the Reed rancho. Strawberry jam . . ."

Fowler nodded his head at the recollection. "Mighty tasty," he agreed, "but I'd like to have that chicken fried and served up with a mess of biscuits. What say, Andrew? Do you favor the cooking of lower California or the lower Arkansas?"

"I approve of both your choices," I said, my stomach voicing its agreement. "But as for me, give me a piece of beefsteak."

Our imaginary feast was interrupted by an unpleasant, unexpected arrival. A horseman riding at top speed descended the bank of the stream across from us and splashed headlong into the creek. Dog jumped up, barking fiercely, his ruff raised stiffly above his shoulders.

The rider that clattered noisily into our camp was Patrick Dunn. He rode in with his revolver drawn and leveled in our faces. "Call off that wolf, Sinnickson," he demanded, "or I'll shoot him down."

We were nowhere close to our stacked rifles. I let my fingers creep down to the coiled whip hanging from my belt. Out of the corner of my eye, I saw Tor Fowler drop his hand from his knee to the top of the boot where two inches of knife hilt protruded.

At that tense moment, two more riders appeared at the back of our camp. "Not this time, Sinnickson. I told you there'd be other hands dealt. Move your hands up slowly and keep them in plain sight." It was Jack Powers. To the other man with him, Powers ordered, "Ed, get their weapons."

"Hold on there!" Fowler demanded. "Who are you, and what's this all about?"

"We're looking for a pack mule that belongs to Patrick here," Powers said. "It was stolen from him."

"Well, just open yore eyes, you no-good highbinder. Do you see a mule critter in this here camp?"

Powers grudgingly admitted that he did not. "But I know Sinnickson's type. Jew name, Sinnickson?" His ruddy cheeks glowed with a delighted sneer. "You'd figure a Heb for a sneak thief, right, boys?"

Fowler's fists clenched, and the line of his jaw tightened. From the look in his eye, I could tell he was fixing to remove the saddle from Powers' horse without having Powers get off first.

"Leave it," I said. "It's not worth getting shot over."

"Smart Jew-boy, huh?" Patrick Dunn laughed.

Patrick's brother Ed took my whip and Fowler's boot knife, then moved crabwise around our camp to the stacked rifles. He had a .50-caliber hogleg in his hand for protection against dangerous folks like us, but it seemed to me that he kept its muzzle and his attention focused on Dog. Dog was still bristled and growling low in his throat.

"Well, I guess we can't hang you for mule thieves today," Powers said, leaning heavily on the last word. "But we can't leave without correcting this unlawful claim."

"What's that supposed to mean?" I said.

Powers rubbed his gun hand through his swept-back silvery-gray hair. "I see you've illegally claimed more of this stream than you're entitled. How'd you ever think you'd get away with claiming three claims for only two men?"

"We've got three partners. One claim for each partner, just like the mining regs say."

Powers pretended to look around and scan the hillsides while Patrick Dunn laughed loudly. Ed joined in the laughter, but his had a nervous quality.

"Three partners? I only see two broken-down miners and one no-account half-breed boy. Don't you know that Injuns can't hold claims?"

"Joaquin worked his claim, same as us," I said.

Powers shook his head in mock sympathy. "Pity you don't get to town more often," he said. "There have been some changes made. I'll wager your claim isn't even registered properly."

"Registered!" Fowler exploded. "Our stakes are up, plain as day!"

59

"So they are," Powers noted. "Ed, Pat, take care of that." Patrick Dunn whooped and rode around the claim, ripping out our stakes and hurling them on our campfire. He threw a loop of rope around the rocker, then dragged it over on its side. Galloping a ways downstream, the bouncing and bumping cradle held its own till he ran it up against a boulder and it splintered to pieces.

So much rage and frustration boiled up in me then that the bitter taste of hot bile rose into my mouth. It felt like an animal caught in a steel-jawed trap, to be taken unawares and forced to stand by while our camp was destroyed. My face must have shown the anger for it was Tor's turn to caution me. "Steady, Andrew," he muttered, "for the sake of the boy."

Patrick Dunn proceeded to retrieve his loop, then dropped it over our tent pole. Another whooping gallop and the canvas was ripped to pieces. Our belongings were scattered and most ended up sunk in the stream.

Powers nodded his approval, while Ed Dunn looked on and agitatedly fingered his revolver. When Patrick returned, he made as if to toss his noose over Joaquin's head. Caution all gone, I had my shout for Dog and leap for Ed's gun all planned when Powers called it off.

"Leave him be, Pat," he said. Then to me he remarked, "I guess this about evens the score, eh, Sinnickson?"

Ed threw whip, knife, and rifles in the creek, then mounted his horse, and the three rode off up the stream. We watched them out of sight, then set to gathering the demolished camp into some kind of order again. All the time I was thinking how Powers was right about this hand, but after this the game was still far from over.

CHAPTER 6

We had intended to work the claims until our supplies ran out in a few weeks. The encounter with Jack Powers and the Dunn brothers changed our plans. Beans and hardtack destroyed; precious cornmeal trampled in the mud. After putting our camp back into some kind of order, we surveyed the wreckage and decided that if we wanted to eat, we had to head for Angel's Camp pronto. Fortunately, we had not been robbed. We kept our gold dust in a two-quart canning jar tucked away in the hollow stump of an old oak tree on the bank of the creek. Every evening after dark we had made deposits at our "bank." Now we figured it was time for a withdrawal.

We divided three hundred dollars in gold dust equally between the three of us.

Tor hefted his share with satisfaction. "Beats herdin' cows, now don't it, boys? Let's see . . . at two dollars a hide it peers to me I'm carryin' fifty cattle in this here poke. Yessir, it shore do beat anythin' I ever seen b'fore!"

I had to agree with him on that. We had pulled more out of the Calaveras in one month than I could have made from my little herd in two years. Joaquin, who had worked as hard at the claim as a grown man, never imagined that he would possess so much wealth! One hundred dollars in gold would buy him passage on a schooner to Hawaii and a real education in the mission school. Schooling was the only way to answer ignorant bullies like Jack Powers and the Dunn brothers. One day, I explained to Joaquin, he might return to California as a man of learning. A judge, perhaps. Or maybe governor of the whole state. He could spit in the eye of any bigot and say his success began along a ten-foot stretch of Calaveras Creek!

The thought of overcoming skunks like Jack Powers fired the boy's imagination. Remembering the tales of Mr. Ames about Hawaii, he gazed far to the west, as though he could already see himself at home among the brown-skinned Sandwichers on their island. I resolved to speak with Ames on the matter of Joaquin's schooling at the first opportunity. Eagerly, the boy placed his poke in my care, asking only that he might have one pinch of the stuff to purchase a jar of jam when we returned to Angel's Camp.

Having been absent from Angel's Camp for a month, however, I had no idea just how much gold dust it would take to buy even a small jar of jam.

The place had sprawled out four times bigger than when we left. Canvas tents, fashioned from the sails of abandoned ships, sprouted like mushrooms on both sides of the creek. The streets were mud bogs crisscrossed here and there by logs with the bark still on them. Crudely lettered signs hung above the tent flaps, bearing the names of stores and saloons and cafes and even a barbershop. The tinkle of banjo music drifted up to the rise as we looked down in wonder at the transfiguration. I rubbed a hand over the coarse black beard that sprouted below my hawk's beak nose and eyed the huge oak barrel painted to resemble a fat barber pole.

"A shave," I said, remembering hot towels and clean lather of a distant life.

"Fried chicken." Tor tugged his long whiskers and cocked an eye at the ragged sign outside a ragged tent advertising HOME COOKING.

"Strawberry jam," cried the newly wealthy Joaquin, licking his lips and pointing straight to the big sign above the AMES DRY GOODS AND SUNDRIES. "Just like the kind Señora Reed makes!"

The waters of the Calaveras were brown and murky from the work and traffic of hundreds of men. The shantytown was hardly more than a pest hole, but to each of us it was a vision of civilization, comfort, and luxury. All of these things were to be bought for a price. As we were soon to discover, even small luxuries were worth their weight in gold!

The dry goods store of Mr. Ames was crammed into a tent created from the weathered canvas of a square-rigged ship. The ship was owned by the Ames Trading Company in Honolulu and had sailed to San Francisco stuffed full of merchandise and Hawaiian workmen. It was Ames's plan to dismantle the vessel and build a proper store from its timbers in San Francisco that winter. Meanwhile, a second schooner from the islands would keep the San Francisco company well supplied with Yankee broadcloth and all the goods the tribe of miners would desire. The tent in Angel's Camp was the forward outpost for what the little Yankee saw as a thriving empire of commerce. Three wagonloads of supplies had arrived the day before, and the tent was crammed with crates of merchandise stacked from floor to ridgepole. Miners crammed the space between the boxes, shouting at Ames for the price of blankets or boots or shovels.

Tor scowled in at the mob through the tent flap. "Looks to me like Ames is near to having a riot on his hands. Ain't so shore I'm up to a fresh brawl without a bite to eat first."

Joaquin grimaced as he saw two miners inside wrestling over a shovel. One had drawn a blade halfway from his belt when the two men were forcibly separated by an enormous dark-skinned Kanaka, whose bushy black hair brushed the canvas ceiling of the tent. I estimated that the Hawaiian was over six and a half feet tall and thick as an old oak tree. He made even my six-foot one-hundred-eighty-pound frame feel small. His features were coarse, and he scowled like a bouncer in a bawdy house. Such a savage face and enormous stature drove all thought of their quarrel from the minds of the two arguing customers. Both released the shovel and stepped back as if they had just met a grizzly bear face-to-face. At this moment

Ames parted the crowd and appeared like King Solomon to resolve the matter. We remained outside the store and watched the event through the flap.

"Well done, Boki," Ames congratulated the Hawaiian, then raised his hands to the crowd, which now lapsed into respectful silence. "Now listen up," Ames instructed the men. "No arguments in my store or Boki here will crack your skulls and throw you out in the street. I run a respectable, law-abiding dry goods store. No guns, knives, clubs, or fists will be allowed. You want my merchandise, you'll act civilized."

"But that there is the last shovel!" cried a mud-caked miner from the back of the tent. "I been diggin' with my cook pot. When you gonna get more shovels in?"

"I grabbed that there shovel first," cried one of the grizzly combatants. "Then he come along and —" His hand returned to the hilt of his knife, and Boki snatched him up by the scruff of his neck. Before we could say howdy, Boki tossed that man out the tent flap. He flew by us and landed spraddle in the mud. It appeared that Boki was the law for the time being. Men shuffled and sniffed and looked down at the toes of their boots. I had seen such looks on the faces of guilty schoolboys caught smoking behind the barn.

"Well, gentlemen?" cried little Ames from beneath the shadow of his giant. "What's it to be? You get in line or Boki gives you the boot. There ain't a place between here and Boston has what

66

we got to sell. The line forms there." He pointed at the tent flap and at us. His eyes lingered on us for a moment, and then his pinched face broke into a grin as the mob broke up and formed a line back out the tent and into the mud of the street. "Well, now!" he cried. "Well! Well! My friends! My friends!" He gathered us in even as his scowling customers shuffled into line. "You're back early by my reckoning. You struck it rich then? Come in to spend a little jack at my humble establishment?"

"We come to spend a little all right," I said in wonder at the scene before me. "Although it 'peers to me that you're the one who's struck it rich."

"A gold mine," he agreed, mussing the hair of Joaquin and thumping Dog on the head. "Anything a man could need right here. Everything a man could want . . . or nearly . . . if he's willing to pay for it." He nudged the toe of my ragged boot. "Three dollars for your road stompers go for forty dollars up here. Ee-yup. You in the market, Andrew?" His eyes glinted with amusement as I blinked back at him in astonishment.

"That's near half my poke!" cried Tor, clutching the little bag of gold dust in his coat pocket.

Someone mumbled behind me. "Ten dollars he charges for a fifty-cent shovel."

Then another surly grumble, "One dollar fer one onion. Figure that."

Ames cheerfully replied, "Onions all the way from the Sandwich Islands, lads."

"Mighty expensive sandwiches they make, too," Tor muttered.

Ames rubbed his hands together. "Well, lads," he said to us. "What'll it be? Seeing how you saved my life, I'll take you to the head of the line."

I figured that I had just enough to buy a sack of onions if that was what I had in mind. I shook my head, knowing that we would have to recalculate what provisions we could afford to buy.

Joaquin looked hopefully into the face of the storekeeper. "Please, señor. I have been dreaming of Señora Reed's strawberry jam. You have jam, Señor Ames? I have a dollar to spend."

Overhearing the child, someone called back, "An ounce of jam is an ounce of gold dust, kid. Ain't you heard the rules for half-breeds around here?"

Ames whirled around. "Who said that?" he demanded. "Boki! What lowdown skunk thinks he's going to set the prices in my store?"

Boki pointed down at a red-shirted fellow holding a sack of beans. "This one," Boki replied in a surprisingly soft, melodious voice.

"Beans you're buying?" Ames menaced. "Ain't you heard the price of beans for dirty-bearded fellows wearing red shirts has gone up? That'll cost you one pound of dust for every pound of beans. Put up or get out!"

With Boki to back him up, Ames could set his own prices. And if he wished, he could even choose to sell a quart of precious jam to a boy for a pinch of gold dust. This is exactly what Ames decided to do.

As the offended miner tossed down the sack of beans and stalked out, Ames growled, "He's one of Jack Powers' gang. Skunks, all of them. Even if he paid me a pound of gold for a pound of vittles, I'd rather not sell to the likes of him."

And so it was that we discovered that Ames and Angel's Camp had become unhappily acquainted with Jack Powers while we had been gone.

"Jack Powers is the very reason we've come into town early," I explained.

"Him and the Dunn brothers wrecked our camp." Tor eyed the retreating gang member. "We ain't et in a while."

At that, Ames left the store in the capable hands of Boki and two other Hawaiians and led the way through the mire to HOMECOOKING CAFE. Joaquin followed after bearing his jar of strawberry jam.

The proprietor of the Homecooking Cafe was a rotund, heavy-jowled man, whose bald knob of a head was enclosed by a fringing thicket of bristling gray hair. He had a canvas apron tied high up across his chest, and while we approached the front of his establishment, he was transferring another layer of grease from his hands to the cloth.

Tor whispered to me over my shoulder "Pay it no mind, Andrew. It don't appear that his cookin' has hurt him none!"

The owner beamed as he greeted us. "Welcome, gents. Mister Ames. Sit down, sit down."

We seated ourselves on a variety of what passed for chairs — two empty crates, the top half of a cracker barrel and an old trunk. Two rough plank tables ran the complete length of the tent and completed the dining arrangements.

"What'll you have?"

"Now yore talkin'," Tor said eagerly. "Fried chicken for me."

The man shook his head. "Sorry, I can't oblige. We ain't got no chicken."

"Biscuits?" asked Joaquin hopefully, waving the jar of jam.

The host of the Homecooking Cafe thrust out his lower lip and folded his arms across the grease-stained apron. "Nope."

Fowler sounded a touch testy when he said, "Wal now, why don't you just tell us what you do have 'stead of us guessin'."

"Beef or beans," was the response.

We three partners looked at one another while Ames watched us with amusement. "No beans," I replied for the group. "How's the beef?"

"Excellent choice! Four steaks, coming up." He gave Ames a broad wink and departed toward the back flap of the tent. As he passed through we could see a black cook tending a steaming pot next to an open fire. A dressed beef carcass was hanging just beyond the fire. "Mose!" the owner shouted at his cook, "throw four more slabs on the grill!"

"Just like Mama used to make," Fowler observed wryly.

Despite the disappointing news about the menu, we were pleased with the prospect of heartier fare than we had eaten in weeks. I took some ribbing on account of my preference being the only choice available, but it was all in fun.

The wait while our dinner was being cooked gave Ames a chance to catch us up on the news of the camp. "Some Mexican fellas from down Sonora way found a seven-pound chunk of gold and quartz. Figures to be worth five hundred dollars, maybe more. How you three doing?"

I was a little chagrined when I answered. "We thought we were doing all right, but after looking at the prices of things —" I stopped so as not to offend Ames, but he only grinned and said that he knew, and weren't the prices ridiculous. I went on then, "Anyway, I guess we're making expenses."

"I told you that it was easier finding gold in miners' pockets than in the streams hereabouts," Ames said forthrightly. Then his face darkened. "But I sell honest goods. There's many who deal in second-rate, cheap-john — weevily flour and salt pork that would have gagged General Washington's men at Valley Forge."

"Jack Powers, for instance?" I asked.

"Ah, Powers!" Ames almost spat out the name. "He sits in his tent gambling and scheming like a spider in a web. Make no mistake — his influence runs deep hereabouts. He's made a pile from the crooked card games he's staked and from watered-down Who Hit John in saloons that look to him for protection."

"Is he so hard to read that folks haven't got him figgered?" Tor asked. "Seems to me he'd be

71

run outta most places."

Ames shook his head. "There's a class of men in the diggings who work one day and then go to hunting easier ways to fill their wallets. Powers caters to them . . . stakes them to drinks and meals in exchange for their support. He rallies them around causes he favors, like running foreigners off their claims over trumped-up charges so he can take them over and sell them to some greenhorn."

The tent flap gapped open again, and a heaping platter of sizzling beefsteak was propelled into the room by the smiling owner. The trencher on which the seared meat rested was a salvaged barrelhead, but little we minded that. The aroma that accompanied the sight of our meal set our mouths to watering and stomachs to rumbling.

The proprietor set the platter down with a flourish, and the plank table actually groaned under the weight. "That'll be an ounce," he said as we grinned at each other in anticipation, *"each."* Our grins turned to grimaces of consternation.

Fowler's eyes were fixed on the topmost steak, and when he spoke it appeared that he was addressing his words to the chunk of meat. "Fifteen dollars? That's highway robbery."

The owner of the Homecooking Cafe looked ready to snatch the serving dish back out of jeopardy when Ames spoke up. "It's all right, John. This meal is on me."

Smiles erupted on all our faces, including the host. "Mighty nice of you, Mister Ames, considering that you already supplied the beef."

72

"What'd he mean?" Tor asked after the owner had gone to greet some newly arrived customers. "Are you in the cattle business, too?"

I was eagerly slicing into my steak. I did not care who had raised the beef or sold it or cooked it. All I wanted to do was eat it. I noticed how dull my hunting knife was behaving and made a mental reservation to see to sharpening it.

"You might say I'm in the cattle business," Ames said. "I sold John a spare team of oxen after my load of provisions got here."

"You don't say," I mumbled around an especially chewy hunk of steak. I saw Tor's jaw muscles working away, and Joaquin seemed to be in particular concentration over his portion.

"Yessir," Ames went on, "at these jewelry prices for meat, I wished I could get my hands on a whole herd."

Fowler, Joaquin, and I all stopped mid-chew and stared at each other. "Do you," I mumbled, having to shift the load to the other side of my cheek. "You mean to say an old cow critter like this that was leather clear through his middle sells for fifteen dollars a steak?"

Ames nodded.

Fowler worked his quid of gristle around till it was safe to swallow, and then inquired, "What does that figger out to on the hoof?"

"Well, John paid me a hundred apiece for the team, but real beefstock would fetch more. Why? Do you boys know where you can get your hands on a herd?"

"Right here!" said Joaquin, bouncing up. "Señor Ames, Senor Andrew is a ranchero. He owns a herd *himself.*"

"Could it be?" I wondered aloud to Tor. "Could we have had the makings of our fortune right under our noses all along?"

"And Don Will Reed," Fowler added. "Don't forget him. He'll be wantin' to throw in with us when he hears about this."

"But is it possible?" I wondered aloud. "Nobody's ever driven a herd up from southern California before. Not that I ever heard tell of anyway. Could we do it?"

Fowler looked me square in the eye and here is what he said, "How much you figure your herd is worth for hides?" and then, "What's two hundred head times a hundred dollars each figger out to?"

Joaquin whooped and started dancing around the table chanting, "A hundred a head! A hundred a head!" Fowler joined him in an impromptu Virginia reel. The ruckus was so tremendous that John and the cook both hurried inside to see if we were tearing up the place.

CHAPTER 7

I was pacing back and forth in front of the tent flap. My mind was a whirl of calculations: distances from one river crossing to the next, where we could find the best feed along the way, how many vaqueros we would need. A sudden flurry of noise from the street outside the Homecooking Cafe drew my attention.

Almost involuntarily I stepped through the canvas opening to see what was up. My thoughts were really three hundred miles away, so it took a few moments for what I was seeing to register with me.

Patrick Dunn was riding into town, and he had a prisoner in tow. The description is exact because the man, a tall fellow in South American garb, stumbled on foot at the end of a rope attached to Dunn's saddle. The prisoner's hands were tied together in front of him, and he fought to keep his balance in the slimy mud of the roadway. Patrick's brother Ed followed along behind, leading a pack mule.

Apparently the capture had not gone altogether smoothly. Patrick Dunn's left eye was swollen shut, and Ed had what looked like a knife slash across his right forearm.

A circle of babbling and angry-sounding miners

accompanied the trio, and when Patrick pulled up in front of a gambling tent, the crowd flowed around the scene like a tide of muddy flannel. As the hubbub grew, more prospectors dropped their tools or their liquor bottles or their cards and joined the audience.

Patrick Dunn got off his horse and called into the gambling establishment for Jack Powers. "Mister Powers, sir. We caught him."

Dunn spoke as respectfully as if he were addressing a judge in a New York courtroom. Here in the Sierras, the judge was self-appointed and his bench was an overturned crate marked *Johnson's Baking Soda*. His honor's muddy boots rested in the churned Calaveras clay, and the heavily bearded spectators in their worn dungarees hardly made for a respectable legal setting.

In contrast, the prisoner at the bar was a tall, haughty-looking man. He was wearing a dark brown woolen poncho, banded across the ends with stripes of blue and yellow. The serape was secured around his middle with a six-inch-wide leather belt.

Below the flat-crowned, stiff-brimmed hat were the features of a man more accustomed to giving orders than of being ordered about. He looked more capable of sitting in judgment on all the rest of the assembly than the other way around.

The man's appearance was bruised and puffy, and a once straight nose was canted to the side. His cheeks were stained with gore, and his wrists were raw and dripped blood from the hemp cords.

The contrast between the florid-faced Bowery toughs and this man of proud bearing was ludicrous in the extreme. But the circumstances themselves were no laughing matter.

In the diggings, even petty thievery was not tolerated. A first offense, no matter how slight, was punished severely. The theft of money or mining equipment merited fifty lashes or branding or disfigurement of the ears or nose. Second-time offenders were summarily hanged.

The rules were even tougher for the theft of a horse or pack animal. All a man's possessions and, in fact, his wherewithal to survive in the wilds were transported on the back of some four-footed beast. It meant that death was the standard punishment for being caught once.

I moved closer so as to hear the proceedings.

"Good work, Pat," Powers praised his lieutenant. "Caught him with the evidence, eh?"

"Yessir, Mister Powers. This greaser was actually leading the mule when we caught up with him. Put up a fight too and tried to stab Ed there with a knife."

The tall prisoner addressed Powers in refined Spanish. "If you are the alcalde, señor, you will instruct these ruffians to release me at once! I am Guillermo Navarro, lately of Buenos Aires. My family fled to Chile to escape the tyrant Rosas. I am in California to recoup —"

"Patrick," Powers sneered, "shut that gibberish up, will you?"

"Gladly," Dunn said, and he cuffed the still-bound Navarro with a backhand across the mouth. The unexpected blow staggered the prisoner and silenced him, but his eyes blazed with a fierce hatred.

"Just a minute," I said, shouldering my way between two stocky miners. "Does he get a say in this or no?"

Powers looked mighty displeased at the interruption. I believed then and still do that he actually understood some of Navarro's words. But with the Spanish-speakers cowed into silence, Powers anticipated no opposition to watching the scene play out according to his own script.

Looking me over thoughtfully, Powers remarked, "Choosing to side against your own kind again, are you, Sinnickson? A man could get a bad reputation doing that too often around here." A tumble in the crowd told me that the story of the attack on the Miwoks had changed some in the retelling.

Powers went on. "Or maybe thieves of all colors *are* more *your* kind, eh, Sinnickson?" He laid a lot of stress on my name when he pronounced it.

"Just hear him out," I said. "This man comes from a wealthy, high-class family in his homeland." To Navarro I said, "Go ahead, señor. I will translate for you."

Navarro inclined his head in a nod of appreciation and resumed his speech. "I came to California to recover my family's lost fortune. When I located a claim and established my camp, I discovered that I needed cash for supplies more than

I needed a mule. So I sold the mule to —" Here he stopped and pointed at Patrick Dunn. I explained to the crowd what had been said so far.

"He sold it to me all right," growled Dunn, "but how did he get the mule back again? Ask him that."

I put this question to Navarro, who shrugged and replied, "When I awoke yesterday, the mule was grazing again near my camp. He must have broken free and returned to the last place that he regarded as home."

When I translated this, there was a general stir in the crowd. Nothing definite, just a clearing of throats, shuffling feet — that sort of thing.

I judged that a number of the onlookers were inclined to believe Navarro's story. What is more, his calm manner while telling his side spoke well for him. For a man facing death, he looked neither shifty nor cringing. He spoke uprightly, like one with truth on his side.

Powers scowled. It was not in his interests to have his bully-boys lose face in front of the miners. To Patrick Dunn, Powers said, "How was the mule secured when you had him last?"

"Tied up tight to a picket line and hobbled."

"And what did you find in the morning?"

"The hobbles were slashed off and the lead rope was cut!"

"Hold on!" I said. "Does anyone else vouch for this?"

"Are you calling me a liar?" Patrick roared. "Taking a stinking greaser's word over mine!"

Here Powers chose to appear judicious, even

fair. "It's a good question, Patrick," he said. "Can anyone support your story?"

"Sure," Dunn bellowed. "My brother saw it, same as me. Ain't that right, Ed?"

Ed Dunn looked at his boots and mumbled something that no one could hear.

"What was that?" Powers demanded. "Speak up."

Talking quickly, as if in a hurry to get it over with, Ed said, "It's the truth." He shot Navarro a momentary look that had emotions I could not read, then went back to staring at his feet. He rubbed his left hand over and over his wounded right arm.

"Hang the greaser!" shouted a voice to my left.

"Stinkin' foreigners makin' off with all our gold and stealin' too!"

"What are we waitin' for? Hang him now!"

"String him up!"

"Wait!" I yelled. "How do you know —" Then I stopped, since I could not make my voice heard over the crowd.

I laid hold of my whip handle. I figured I could clear a space around Navarro long enough to buy him some time.

A calloused grip caught my wrist and yanked my hand away from the lash. The fiercely bearded face of the man named Cannon thrust into my own. "Not this time, Sinnickson!" he roared, then something crashed into the back of my head, and I dropped like a stone.

How long I lay unconscious in the filth of the Angel's Camp street, I don't know. Not long perhaps, for they told me later that what followed took only a minute or two at most.

When I woke up, my head was ringing like two dozen blacksmiths were hammering inside it. When I started to stand, the best I could manage was to get up on one elbow.

In front of me, not twenty yards away, dangled the lifeless body of Guillermo Navarro. He was hoisted into eternity at the end of a rope slung over an oak limb. All around the street was deserted. Even Powers and his vermin had disappeared.

Joaquin came running to me, followed by Fowler and, more slowly, Ames and Boki. "Señor Andrew," Joaquin gasped, "are you all right?"

"Just help me up," I slurred. My next look went to Fowler. I wanted to ask him where he had been, why he had not come to help. He saw and answered my unspoken questions.

"I'm awful sorry, Andrew," he said, biting his words off short. "This big feller held me back." He stabbed his thumb at Boki's massive girth. "He grabbed me from behind and sat on me."

I gave Boki a look of anger and reproach, but it was Ames who answered for him. "Don't be blaming Boki, Andrew," he said. "I told him to keep Tor back, and I held on to the boy myself. Yessir, and a mighty good thing too. If you three had interfered, they'd have hanged all of you, sure."

CHAPTER 8

The ground was pocked with places where prospectors had dug in search of gold, then abandoned. Heaps of brown earth and broken rocks made the clearing look as if it were a colony of giant ants instead of a graveyard. Soil barren of gold was the only ground fit for burying the dead miners of the Calaveras gold fields.

Wood planks were too precious to use for building a coffin, and so we cut down the body of Guillermo Navarro and wrapped him in a red woolen blanket for burial. He was carried to his makeshift grave on the shoulders of half a dozen of his countrymen. Only another dozen Spanish speakers joined the solemn procession up the hill. Tor and I followed behind with Joaquin. Ames, who provided the shroud, came after with Boki. There were no other mourners. Those who might have come under different circumstances were too frightened by what they had witnessed to associate themselves with the proud and noble Navarro even at his graveside.

"I assume he was a Catholic gent," said Ames as they laid Navarro's body in the damp hole.

There was no priest for a hundred miles. The sad fact that the dead man would be launched into eternity without a decent burial distressed each of his comrades. They looked sadly from man to man and asked who would say the proper words for their friend. There was no one to speak. None who knew how to pray. There was not a copy of the Good Book among them. Hats in hand they simply gazed over the rim of the grave at the body.

I understood their language well and explained to Ames and Boki the problem. "Easy enough to cut him down and put him in the ground, but there isn't a one of them who knows what to say. No Scriptures to read from, I reckon."

Tor furrowed his brow. "It ain't fittin' a feller to git hisself hung without reason and then can't git hisself buried proper on the same day. You go on, Andrew. Say somethin', why don't you? You know the words in the Good Book. Go on and say what you know about it."

I had indeed gotten my own schooling fresh out of reading the Good Book. I had not had any primer except Matthew, Mark, Luke, and John. As a child I had hated memorizing scriptures every day, and I had resented the message those words had taught. But I was grown now. Sadder and wiser from living in a world such as this. Long since I had learned that nothing was certain in life from one moment to the next, and that the only thing I could truly count on were those words I had been forced to learn as a child. Yet I hesitated to speak. After all, Navarro was not my companion. I had never met him before the hour of his death. What could I say?

83

The question was answered for me. Tor stepped up and nodded to the small assembly. He spoke in the Spanish language. Truth to tell, his Spanish was much more refined than when he spoke in his own tongue.

"My friends. We are new to your small circle, but in our hearts we are one with you in this tragic hour. Great injustice has happened here, and how are we to answer to it?"

"We have no priest, señor," cried a short man dressed in a poncho similar to that which Navarro had worn. "For us there is no justice. They killed Guillermo only because they wanted his claim and he would not sell it."

"This is true," enjoined another.

There were nods of agreement all around.

The man in the poncho continued. "We are simple men. Guillermo Navarro was a great man among us in our homeland. What can we say to put his soul at peace? If it was one of us in that grave, he would know the words even without a priest. He once studied for the priesthood but married instead. He is . . . was . . . the father of three young sons. What can we say? Bad men have done this thing to a good man. Where is there justice? Where is God that He would allow such a thing?"

"Well, Andrew?" Tor questioned me. "You know the Book backward and forward. Can you speak to this?"

"It isn't my place," I replied in English.

Tor did not accept my answer. He put a hand

on my shoulder then addressed the others. "Here is one American who tried to stop the lynching of your friend. He is a learned man and perhaps can speak the words of a priest if you permit —"

A chorus of "Sí! Tell us the words, señor!" erupted from the company while I frantically searched my heart for some answer.

After a time, the group fell silent. Wind scraped the treetops and made a hushed, whispering sound. I looked at the red shroud and then at the rugged hills of the Calaveras, and I prayed that the good Lord would speak not only to the men around me, but also to my own bitter heart as well.

"This place is called Calvary," I began in Spanish. "Named after a place where long ago the one truly innocent man in all the world was murdered." It was cool, but beads of sweat stood out on my brow. I switched into English, for my memories of Scripture flowed better that way, while Tor translated my words for the others. "Seems to me that Jesus who died on Calvary knows just what happened here today. Seems He experienced some of the same as Guillermo Navarro here at the hands of a mob. Folks accused Jesus of things He was not guilty of. Hired guns were paid to bring false testimony against Him. He was tied up and beaten. He was paraded through the streets. His friends were afraid to speak for Him . . . afraid of dying themselves. . . ."

At this a sob erupted from the man in the poncho. He cried out the name of his friend and dropped to his knees on the mound of earth beside the grave. "How can you forgive me, my friend? I should have fought! I should have died with you! Oh, I am a coward! A coward!"

There were others among the group who wept silently and reflected on their own fear and failure. I remembered Peter who had cursed and denied he even knew the Lord, and for just a moment I glimpsed the true meaning of the first Calvary. My own words were not enough.

"It has always happened that men are full of death and darkness. We know the kind of lust that justifies murder and the kind of fear that keeps us from standing up for what is right. We who stand here alive are responsible for the death of an innocent man. No. I do not speak of Navarro. I speak of the One at whose feet Guillermo Navarro now bows. I speak of Jesus, The Innocent, who died at Calvary because your sins and my sins shouted across the ages, 'Crucify Him! Hang Him from a tree!' "

Tears flowed from the eyes of the men as Tor repeated this.

"I have failed!" cried Navarro's friend. "What can I do? What?"

"Remember what Jesus said as He died: 'Father forgive them, for they know not what they do.' He was thinking of this moment when He spoke those words. He was seeing me and you. He was watching the men who hanged Navarro. . . . His friends took Him down and buried Him. They mourned for three days, but then Jesus rose from the dead. He is still alive. He says that one day

86

every knee shall bow and every tongue confess that He is Lord. . . . Those who have loved Him . . . like Guillermo Navarro . . . will see heaven. Those who have denied Him, who have not asked forgiveness for their sins, will wake up one day in hell. All the gold in Calaveras Canyon will not save them. One day they will be dust like your friend, but their eternal souls will wish that it was they who died this day instead of this innocent man. This I believe. The Lord is merciful to those who love Him. His eyes see all things. Pity the men who have done this. Rejoice for Guillermo Navarro, for his place in eternity is forever established. His battle is fought and won and finished on Calvary."

We sang a hymn then and prayed some. Each man knelt and asked forgiveness for their failures and many sins. Each left that barren, desolate place with something new born in his heart. We were forgiven. We somehow had a glimpse of Christ's death for us on faraway Calvary. There was much in my own heart that was forever altered on that terrible day. I knew I would never forget the grief that an innocent man was lynched before my eyes. Something in me cried, "Never again!" No. As long as I had breath in me, I would not stand and see another Calvary. . . .

CHAPTER 9

The aroma of sage and autumn oak leaves mingled with the scent of sea air. As we rode across the vast Santa Barbara rancho of Will Reed, Shawnee seemed to recognize each steer and heifer of my herd. She nodded at the black, slat-sided, long-horned beasts as if to greet them. Perking her ears and nickering softly, she let me know that she was pleased to be home again; pleased to be in familiar pastures with the prospect of doing what she was born to do. As for Dog, he seemed to agree with my sharp little mount. There was a spring to his step as we passed by the herd. His mouth was open in a dog-smile that made Joaquin laugh with pleasure.

"Look, Señor Andrew!" the boy called. "Dog smiles at Señor Toro." He pointed at the rangy steer as the critter raised its head from the dry grass and eyed Dog suspiciously. "And Señor Toro remembers Dog nipping his heels, I think. He seems not too happy that his shaggy master has come back from the gold fields!"

Tor hooted. "Gold on the hoof, Andrew. Reckon that ol' Toro ain't gonna be none too happy when he figgers out Dog is takin' him north to be et up!"

"We just won't tell 'em till it's too late," I enjoined. I did not say so, but it did feel mighty fine seeing those old familiar hides again. Like my horse, I knew I was not born to spend my life grubbing for gold in an icy-cold stream. Herding cattle was something I knew. I had done it when my only prospect was to make two dollars a hide for shoe leather. Now I looked out across the Santa Barbara hills and saw my fortune.

My herd mingled with that of Will Reed's. Since I had purchased them from the Reed rancho, many of my heifers bore Will's leaning R brand. I had added two notches to the right ear of each as well as my own Lazy S brand. Will had given me a good price on those heifers, and I hoped now to return the favor. Had he heard of the hungry miners of the Calaveras? Had he looked out over his thousands of cattle and imagined the worth of his stock? Such a vast herd could feed every one of the prospectors in the north this year and for many years to come.

Tor tugged his beard thoughtfully as he eyed the grazing beasts of the hillsides. "Andrew," he ventured cautiously. "You ain't got but two hunert cattle. Now that's more'n I got, which makes you a rich man."

"We're partners, Tor. Didn't you come looking for me when you heard about the gold strike?"

"It didn't exactly work out the way I figgered."

"Sure it did. We just found a different sort of gold. We're partners, and there's the end of it."

He nodded slowly. "What are we fixin' to do

after we sell this bunch? I mean . . . they're fine fer a start. But I don't fancy bein' a rancher for a month and then goin' out of business."

I had spent the miles considering this very problem and had come up with a plan. "I've got it all figured out, partner," I said as we topped the rise and the white frame home of Will Reed came into view below us.

At first glance the place seemed exactly as it had when we left it. The two-story white New England-style home seemed out of place in the midst of the brown, oak-studded valley. I had heard once that Will had seen a picture of just such a house when he was a young man. After his marriage to Francesca he had ordered every plank, nail, and window from Boston and had them shipped around the Horn. Will Reed was a man who put muscle and action to his dreams. I hoped that he would do the same when he heard my plan.

The rubble of an old adobe cookhouse lay where it had fallen during the quake of '46. Smoke rose from the chimney of the new wood-frame cookhouse, and we caught the scent of bacon on the breeze. Tor raised his face to the aroma and patted his belly. "Been dreamin' of Simona's bacon and biscuits. I'd of given a bag of gold dust just for a bite of her cookin'!" He urged his mount to a slow canter down the gently sloping lane.

The sun glinted on the red hair of two young men as they strolled out of the barn and looked toward our dust.

"By the color of their hair, that'll be two of Will's boys, I reckon," Tor remarked as I rode at his side. "He's got hisself a whole litter of red-headed younguns. I ain't met but a few since most is in Hawaii at school. These'uns must be just returned."

At this information, Joaquin's face brightened. He leaned forward in his saddle as though to look more closely at the two Reed brothers. I lifted my hand in greeting. A tentative wave replied. As we came nearer I saw that the older brother was perhaps fifteen or sixteen years old. The younger was little more than Joaquin's age — twelve or thirteen. They could not have finished their term at the mission school in Hawaii. Why, then, had they come home to California? I felt a vague sense of uneasiness at that thought. Had some family tragedy come upon the peaceful rancho in our absence? Was Will all right? Francesca?

Truth to tell, the rancho seemed too quiet. Normally the barns and corrals were a swarm of activity. Vaqueros came and went with unbroken regularity. The only people in sight this morning were the two brothers, who eyed our approach with evident suspicion.

"Where is everyone?" I wondered aloud.

"It ain't Sunday. Ain't in church," Tor responded, scanning the hills and herds beyond. He pointed toward two vaqueros on the rise bringing in strays. Weeks before, there would have been a dozen hanging around the cookhouse waiting for the dinner bell.

91

"Somethin's up, Andrew," Tor said. "Mebbe this ain't gonna be as easy as we figgered."

There was an odd, deserted air about the place. Too many cattle. Not enough vaqueros. I remembered the tales we had heard of the sailors deserting their ships and leaving them to rot in San Francisco Bay while entire crews struck out for the gold fields. Could that be happening here as well?

At that instant, the tall, muscular form of Will Reed appeared in the opening of the barn. His eldest son, Peter, joined him a moment later. I knew Peter well from the days of the Bear Flag revolt. Nineteen years old now, Peter was as tall as his father and as strong as a grizzly. He recognized my piebald horse instantly and shouted my name.

"Andrew!"

Will laughed at the sight of us, as though he had known all along that we would be back soon. We were a grubby-looking bunch. The best bath we had managed was a dip in the Rio Bravo three days before.

"Home from the gold fields so soon?" Will greeted us with an edge of amusement in his voice. "Struck it rich already, have you?"

Interest sparked on the faces of the younger brothers. They eyed us with open curiosity.

"What I want to know, Will Reed," Tor grinned and eyed the smoke from the cookhouse chimney, "we ain't missed breakfast, have we?"

One platter was heaped high with fried eggs;

a mountain of bacon was piled on the other. Fresh melons, warm tortillas, butter and strawberry jam were all washed down with cool buttermilk and coffee with thick cream.

We ate the feast as though we had not eaten anything at all since we left. Simona cocked a disapproving eye at Tor as she placed another plate of eggs in front of him. His mouth was too stuffed to say thanks, and he grunted like a hog at the trough.

Simona scowled at Tor and opened her mouth as if to scold him, but Francesca silenced her with a stern look. "Our guests will be needing more bacon, Simona. See to it, por favor."

I always said that Francesca Reed was a first-class lady. She ignored the fact that we seemed to have forgotten our table manners, but all the while she kept her sons eating proper by just raising an eyebrow at the three of them. Napkins in place, silverware held just so; they said their "please and thank you, ma'am" and "will you pass the butter" like proper gentlefolk, while we stuffed our grizzly faces. Peter, James, and John they were called, and they were just as polite as apostles, too. Will and Francesca kept them from asking questions until we three were working on our second platesful of food. Joaquin wiped his mouth on his sleeve and blew his nose on his napkin.

"Mother?" John muttered in disgust, as if he did not care to share breakfast with the half-starved, half-breed boy across the table from him. The thought crossed my mind that I had neglected the boy's upbringing in some ways. I was about to send Joaquin out to eat in the cookhouse when Francesca intervened.

"You have had some great adventures in the gold fields, Joaquin?" she asked kindly. Her sons leaned forward attentively, seeming to forget Joaquin's ill manners.

The boy talked around his mouthful of eggs and babbled on about the first gold dust he had panned from the Calaveras. "Plenty of gold, Señora Reed," he said. "But no eggs. You see? The miners are paying one dollar in gold dust to buy even one small egg. I have eaten three weeks of gold dust this morning," he added happily.

"This is true?" Francesca turned to me.

"Yes, ma'am. One dollar for an egg. And a stringy steak is worth a whole ounce of gold," I explained. Tor mumbled confirmation.

"Are they all as hungry as you, then?" Will was amused. "I'm not surprised. A man can't eat gold dust, can he?" He nodded his head at his sons as though he had been telling them this before we brought our tales of hunger and hardship home. "Like I said this morning, boys, every vaquero who lit out of here will be back soon enough. Won't take them long. You'll see. Give them a few weeks scrounging around in the cold water and nothing to eat but hardtack and grizzly bear meat . . . they'll wish they could get their hands on a Leaning R steer."

"Ah-ha!" Tor and I interrupted at the same instant.

"The very thing we came to speak to you about, Will!" I cried, mindful that the subject had come first from him.

Will nodded, not yet comprehending my meaning. "I'll wager you've met up with more than one of my men up there. Seventy-five of the best vaqueros in the country . . . two thirds of my men . . . just bolted one night and left us short-handed during branding time. I'll not wish them luck, but when they come crawling back, I'll put them back to honest employment. Feed them and —"

"Feed them!" I cried, perhaps too eagerly. "The very thing!"

It was then that I unfolded my great plan for feeding the hungry miners of the gold fields. They were paying real gold for overcooked cart oxen. What would happen if they laid eyes on the Leaning R brand of Will Reed coming up the trail?

Will let me go on through two more cups of coffee and then jerked me back to reality. "A thousand head, Andrew? Three hundred miles through the tules and the rivers of the big valley?" He shook his head. "It sounds difficult, but possible . . . except for one small detail."

Had I left something out? "What is it?"

"There are no vaqueros left to help you drive the herd." He gave a slight shrug. "My sons have come home from school to help me here on the rancho. There are perhaps two dozen other vaqueros who did not desert. Most have families. They have been on the rancho for several gen-

95

erations. I can't go myself, you see." He gestured toward Francesca, whose baby was due any time. "We cannot spare any more men."

It was Peter who drew himself up and challenged his father's reasoning on this point. "But, Father, if we take one thousand head to the north, that will be one thousand less we have to tend here at the rancho. Could you not spare a few of us for such an enterprise?"

"A few of us?" Will glared down his nose at Peter.

The younger brothers jumped in. "Yes, Father! We can do it! The branding is finished! We managed all of that shorthanded, didn't we?"

I had not spoken of the lawlessness of the gold camps. No word of the murders or lynchings had been mentioned. Nor had the name and evil dominion of Jack Powers been raised. Somehow, however, Francesca Reed sensed that there was much more yet untold of our story. She raised her chin defiantly to her sons. "Your father needs you here," she insisted. "That is all that I shall say on the matter. You are just children. You cannot go to such a place."

John set up a gruff protest. "Children!" he scoffed. "Look at him!" He pointed at Joaquin, who suddenly became a hero. "He is younger than I! He has been there and back! He has a gold claim on the Calaveras River! He has been a partner to Señor Andrew and Señor Tor! Do not call us children, Mother!"

Silence at the table. Will cleared his throat. "I

reckon I was a lot younger than Peter when I
out to come west." He narrowed his eyes
thought. "It was the stuff to make a man of m

"Will?" Francesca warned, seeing the whe
turning in his mind. "They are not you. Pe
is older. Yes. But James and John are . . ."

"Good hands," Will finished. "And I reck
such an adventure might come to a happy co
clusion for them were they to ride at the side
Andrew and Tor. And there is great fortune
be made, even if it is only half as much as Andre
tells us." He turned to me. "I get two dollars
hide for my stock. Ten thousand head are grazin
on my rancho. I will send one thousand to th
north and split the profit with you and Tor. We
can spare Peter, James, and John, and I'll find
vaqueros to make a dozen hands for the drive.
What do you say?"

He put out his hand as the boys whooped and
Francesca looked daggers at all of us. In this way
the deal was set. In our jubilation, we could not
guess that the misgivings of Francesca Reed held
real portent of the danger we were to face in the
coming weeks.

CHAPTER 10

Will Reed chose seven of his remaining vaqueros to accompany his sons and us north. They were not selected because of great skill, he explained, but because they were single men. There were no wives or children to leave behind in their journey.

Were they loyal? Men we could count on? To this Will shrugged his shoulders and replied that these had come to the rancho after nearly every other vaquero had vamoosed at the first rumor of gold. If that was loyalty, then he supposed they were faithful as old dogs.

They were also as mangy looking as old dogs. A scruffier-looking lot I had seldom seen. Alzado, who seemed to tell the others what to do, looked mean enough to top a grizzly bear in a "Who's Uglier" contest. One look at the long knife stuck in his boot top made me rub my throat and think a while about sleeping real light on the journey.

"You need anything done," Will said confidently, "just ask Alzado."

Five other vaqueros — Rodriguez, Garcia, Ramos, Sanchez, and Ortiz — were a close second in appearance and smell to Alzado. The last man on the crew was named Gomez. He was softer than the rest, dressed somewhat cleaner, and

bowed and smiled a lot to Will, his sons, and now to Tor and me as well.

"Pure toady," Tor muttered as Gomez disappeared around the corner of the barn. "Makes me want to wipe my boots off, he does. Give me a tobacco-spittin' grasshopper like Alzado over that smooth, puffed-up toad any day." He shook his head. "Truth to tell, I ain't real sure of any of these fellers, Andrew. I say we take the Reed boys an' you an' me an' Joaquin, and leave these 'uns behind."

I considered the proposal, but a thousand head of cattle meant that we needed more than two grown men and four boys to handle the drive. I reminded Tor of the fact that these seven had remained on the rancho and not jumped ship like their compadres. Tor did not seem comforted by this fact all the same.

It took a week to gather the herd and cut out the young heifers from the steers. Will was not overeager to sell off breeding stock. A wise decision. Keeping his heifers here in the south meant fewer calves in the north. If this was to be a truly profitable enterprise, he said, we had to consider such matters.

All in all, the herd was a much handsomer-looking lot than our vaqueros. Those cows smelled a mite better too, but we put our doubts aside and after a long benediction from the mission priest, we headed out of Santa Barbara.

On the advice of Will, we did not head straight north along the King's Highway that linked the string of missions along the coast. That route was crawling with highwaymen, he told us. Thieves and cutthroats who paid homage to Jack Powers were thick along that way. Even if we managed to drive the herd past them, no doubt word would reach Powers that a thousand head of cattle were moving north on the coast. If the bandit king ever put two and two together, Will rightly said, the herd would be stolen and we would be lucky to escape with *our* hides, let alone the cowhides.

For this reason we chose to drive the herd over the mountains and straight up through the marshy San Joaquin Valley. It was a more difficult journey, to be sure, but the country was inhabited by only a few remaining bands of Yokut Indians. Gentle folk, the Yokuts would pose no threat to us. Tor and I had often remarked how many of them had died off from white man's diseases and the malarial mosquitos brought from the north by French trappers. Taking our herd to the gold fields through the Central Valley might make for a more difficult trip, but at least we would not have to fight men as well as the elements. It was our hope that our arrival in the north would be met by great amazement and hungry miners with pockets filled with gold!

I've never been one to get the wind up easily. I'm not superstitious, nor does the night breeze sighing in the cedars give me the "williwaws," as Tor Fowler would have said. Still, the experience of our first night on the cattle drive did provide ample reason to think that things were not going to be smooth.

One day out of the comforts of Santa Barbara, we were pushing the herd into the narrow defile of Gaviota Pass. The "Canyon of the Seagulls" had come to the world's attention two years earlier, since it was there that the Californios had laid an ambush for Colonel Fremont. You can bet my thoughts went back to those days, because Tor, Will Reed, and I had each had a hand in preventing the success of the trap.

Anyway, on this occasion, with a thousand head of cattle and a largely unknown group of men, I had little time to dwell on past history. Gaviota was still a wild place, with a primitive, dangerous feel to it. Its rocky canyons and steep, narrow trail were favored by outlaws, renegades, and grizzly bears for the waylaying of unwary travelers.

We rolled the herd up for the night into a blind arroyo. We had not pushed as far as I would have liked, but Tor reminded me that cow-critters and men alike both need a little time to settle into a routine. The first passage had to convince both the herd and the vaqueros that it was easier to keep walking forward than to get punished for standing and bellowing to go home.

I posted the first two night herders with instructions to call their relief in two hours. We could have kept more men on watch together, but with the drive all bedded down and placid, there seemed no reason to give up more sleep.

I've heard it said that the toughest watch is the

101

one just before dawn, but in my experience, this is not so. The anticipation of the first glint of gray light along the eastern rim of the world always seemed to sharpen my senses — watching for it, you see.

For me, the hardest part of the dark hours is between two A.M. and four. Seems like every sound is magnified and every worry too. You keep thinking about how far off the daybreak is, and what you most want is to get next to the fire and sleep. There must be something to it, because Pastor Metcalfe always got called out in those hours to attend some poor old soul's shuffle off this mortal coil.

Which is why I assigned myself that shift on purpose. The three Reed brothers took the first watch. They were fast asleep beside the fire when Tor shook me awake at two by the set of the Big Dipper. "Everything all right?" I asked.

"Sure, nice an' quiet. Not even a breeze stirrin'," he said, but with an added comment left hanging in his voice.

"But what?"

"Can't put my finger on it exactly. Peter said there was somethin' in the air durin' his watch. Jest a feelin', he said. Ever'thing near the mouth of the canyon seems settled, but up where the arroyo backs up to the rocks I get an urge to look over my shoulder some."

"Indians, you think?"

"Not likely. Not here. 'Sides, they can read Will Reed's brand, same as us. If they wanted a beef, they'd just sashay in and ask for one. No, it's somethin' else."

"Grizzly?"

Fowler shrugged and yawned. "I'll leave you to it," he said, rolling up in his bedroll. His vaquero partner had already turned in, and Fowler was sawing logs even before I shook Joaquin awake.

I told the boy of Fowler's cautioning words. "Do you wish us to ride with you, señor?" he asked. By "us" he meant him and Dog, who had been sleeping across Joaquin's feet.

"No," I said quietly. "You and Dog sit up here by the fire. I'll ride the circle once and come back."

The farthest back piece of the canyon pinched off against a rock wall, topped by a high, brushy hillside. It was plastered with chaparral and sage and would have made tough going for a limber squirrel, let alone a man on horseback. For that reason, it felt as secure as a corral fence at the rear of the herd, and yet the hairs on my neck prickled.

Shawnee had made no sound to indicate that anything was amiss, but her ears pricked back and forth as if searching for an expected but missing sound. "Easy," I cautioned her. "Let's just sit and look around a spell." No breeze meant no scents on the coolish night air, unless we got up close, so quiet watchfulness was the order of things.

After a time, I was ready to write it off to an uncommon case of the jitters when a steer lying off a ways from the herd caught my attention. Sometimes the lack of movement can be just as telling as a twitch or a wiggle. This animal was lying too flat and too still — dead, without doubt.

I nudged Shawnee up closer. She moved reluctantly as the warm smell of fresh blood reached us both at last. Dark, raking marks stood out on the neck and shoulder of the rust-colored hide, and the corkscrewed position of the head told the rest of the story — mountain lion! Big, smart, and fearless, I judged, from the way he had brought down the steer with a single blow and in complete silence. Of even greater interest to me was the cat's present whereabouts.

The Allen over-and-under was already in my hand, and Shawnee backed away from the kill without being told to. You see, lions prefer to strike from behind, and neither my paint mare nor I intended to give this one any opportunity.

Shawnee walked us very deliberately around the herd in the direction of the fire. We did not want to compound the loss of the steer by flying through the drove in the middle of the night and causing a panic that might end in a stampede. In point of fact, even after reaching the fireside, I did not shout an alarm. Rather, I motioned Joaquin to join me, then roused Tor.

He had the mountain man's knack of coming instantly awake, and after a few words of explanation had a grasp of the situation. "Well, Andrew," he said, peering away from the fire into the dark canyon, "could be a young cat. Mayhap you skeered this here cougar away from his kill."

I shook my head. "Shawnee or I would have

heard him go, the brush being so thick and all."

"Figger yore right . . . which means the other explanation must fit."

"What, Señor Fowler? What does it mean?" asked Joaquin, his eyes round as saucers.

"He means that what we've got is an outlaw lion. A young one might be run off from his prey that easy. An older one would usually stay and fight for it, or else he'd have already drug it off in the brush. But this one didn't do either. He just killed for the sport," I explained.

"And he . . ." Joaquin kind of stuttered and reached out to hug Dog around the neck.

"Right," I agreed. "He'll be back. If we don't deal with him, he'll kill again . . . maybe tonight, maybe tomorrow night . . . but he'll follow the herd till he gets tired of the game."

I saw a shiver start at the base of Joaquin's spine and work its way up till it came out his shoulders with a final shudder. To his credit all he said was, "What do we do about it, Señor Andrew?"

Tor nodded his approval, and I gave the boy a squeeze on his arm. "What *you* need to do," I said, "is stay here with Dog. I don't know if I could keep him from running that cat, and either he'd get hurt or the herd spooked or both."

We woke the Yaqui vaquero by the name of Alzado, which means "warrior." He was a sullen-seeming cuss who grunted more than he spoke, and that but seldom, but he was fearless. Built lean and tough and with all the pride of a people who had never submitted to the Spanish conquest of their homeland, the Yaqui was feared by the others, but much admired too. Out of a band about whom little was known, he seemed the most steady to take out into the darkness to face a rogue lion.

We each took a brand from the fire and again we rode slow and easy back to the spot where I had found the steer. But when we got to the place, there was no carcass to be found. Dismounting, we left the Yaqui holding the horses, while Tor and I scoured the ground. "Could you have mistook the place, Andrew?" Tor asked. "On a dark night such as this, one clump of brush looks pretty like another."

"No," I argued, "I'm certain this was it." We raised the firebrands overhead to give us a wider ring of view. "Look here," I said. "There's blood here on the grass."

I pointed downward at the stain that looked pitch black against the shadowy brush, but Fowler was not watching where I directed. "No doubt yore right," he said, "but in that case he's kilt another one." Fowler's outstretched right arm gestured beyond the glare of the torches some few yards to where another steer's body lay prone on the grass.

It was all I could do to keep from swearing. Not only was this the first night of the drive, but I had scarce been gone ten minutes since viewing the previous victim. It was with relief then that I saw the downed creature move. "Look, Tor," I said. "You're wrong."

We had already taken a few paces in the direction of the animal. Its horned head lifted and pivoted in our direction, wobbling awkwardly as if drunk. That's when we saw the baleful yellow eyes staring back at us over the neck of the steer. In the flickering glow of our burning branches, we watched as a huge cougar raised the head of the dead steer by the grip of his powerful jaws clamped around its throat.

The cat sprang upright, dragging the six-hundred-pound cow as if it were nothing. Tor and I both fired, but our shots took effect only on the dead carcass. The lion flung its prey aside and bounded into the chaparral with a defiant roar and a crash. It was gone for now, but we knew it would be back.

CHAPTER 11

There was no further sleeping done that night. The vaqueros, roused by the sounds of our gunfire, rushed about with some confusion.

The Reed brothers, showing the character typical of their parents, were in favor of setting out on the trail of the big cat at once. Opposing this was the opinion of some others who felt such a plan was *muy malo*, very bad. In fact, Gomez and Rodriguez were ready to call it quits and return to Santa Barbara.

The plan we actually adopted was more cautious than the one but less cowardly than the other. Tor and I formed a picket line of men around the rear of the herd to guard against the lion's return. It was our intention to wait for first light, and then track the animal to where it holed up for the day.

There were no more disturbances, even though we watched until gray dawn reduced the number of visible stars to three. It was a very grumpy group of men who stretched out the kinks and gave up the vigil.

I instructed Peter Reed to ride the point and lead the herd out of the arroyo and up the trail. Tor and I would set out to do the tracking. We were accompanied by the Yaqui, Alzado.

During the night watch, the fawning vaquero Gomez had been one to raise his voice in support of abandoning the drive, but he sang a different tune when the sun came up. "Please, Señor Andrew," he begged, "allow me to accompany you. In my country I am known as a great hunter."

I caught Fowler's raised eyebrow and considered that perhaps the man needed an opportunity to redeem himself, but could not agree. We three would track the cougar till noon, then break off the hunt and rejoin the herd. All the rest were needed for the drive. "No," I said. "You and Joaquin take charge of the remuda."

I planned to return to the point where the puma had bounded away into the darkness, intending to follow the trail of the big cat. Fowler and Alzado set off directly toward a rocky pinnacle that looked to be a likely spot for a den.

"Señor Andrew," Gomez called out, riding after me. "I have something to tell you." He cast a furtive glance toward the pair of riders ahead and noted that Tor and the Yaqui were out of earshot before continuing.

"Not necessary," I said, taking his caution for embarrassment. "I already know what you are going to say."

The vaquero swept off his sombrero with its sugarloaf crown and rubbed his hand across his forehead. "You do?" he asked.

"Sure," I replied. "Don't give it a thought. I don't like my sleep interrupted by a thieving lion, nor a band of hostiles, nor a snake in my bedroll, for that matter."

Gomez stroked his thin, black mustache with a quick, nervous gesture. "Señor is making the joke?" he said.

Now it was my turn to be confused. "What are you driving at, then, if this isn't about last night?"

Gomez reined his palomino alongside. There was a moment's jostling of horses as Shawnee laid back her ears and with bared teeth warned the gelding off from coming too close.

When the stomping settled, Gomez gestured for me to lean over. In a conspiratorial voice he whispered, "It is about the fierce one, the Yaqui."

"Alzado? What about him?"

"He is not to be trusted, señor."

"What do you mean?"

"I have seen him before, señor, in the company of malditos, bad men and robbers. He is hot-tempered and will kill when the mood is on him."

"So?" I said, trying to sound less concerned than I really felt. "Has he made threats against me or mine . . . or you, perhaps?"

Gomez looked as if I'd kicked him in his pride; as if my words cast suspicion on his motives (which of course they did). "Ah no, señor. I only wished to be of service. But if my words are not welcome, then I will keep my own counsel."

"Just see that you keep a sharp eye out for that lion," I said. I pointed downward to a pug mark the size of a horse's hoofprint. "He's big and mean too, and he's been a lot more trouble up to now than Alzado."

110

Gomez drew himself up haughtily and spun the palomino around in the direction of the herd of replacement mounts. As I looked on, Peter Reed shouted the orders that roused the men and the cattle and set both upon the trail. Then I turned to the task of picking my way along the increasingly steep dry wash as it wound up into the wild.

The sun had climbed high in the sky when I reined Shawnee to a halt and reflected on the lion. His tracks had led me on a meandering path, looping in and out of the low hills. Twice I had come upon the bloody remains of other steers killed and dragged into the brush. Three times I lost his trail entirely, having to go back to the last clear print and then ride widening spirals around until I picked up the marks again.

He seemed to have been going nowhere in particular. The commotion around the camp and the shots fired had not scared him into hightailing for home, that much was certain.

Shawnee and I circled another low hill, then were led up to its crest. The barest hint of a crushed place in the weeds showed where the lion had stretched out to take his ease. "What was he playing at?" I remarked to Shawnee. I stood up in the stirrups and found myself gazing out over the canyon where we had spent the night. The dust of the drive had already disappeared, and it was time to think about riding after my herd.

All at once it struck me. Not only had we not scared this particular lion back into the high country, we had not even driven him away from his sport. Or at least not far away. While we had stood guard, he had spent the remainder of the night prowling around our camp, looking for an unprotected way in. While we had been watching for him, he had circled all of us. The thought was enough to give a man the willies.

Tracking him now seemed pointless. We would have to outguess him and get there first, or he would continue to be trouble. I set off into another canyon, toward where I expected to find Tor and the Indian.

Shawnee and I were some little way up a steep hill when we heard the gunshot. I had just turned my head to check my bearings when the ringing echoes bounced down through the canyon, and Shawnee took off as if she had been the bullet fired from the gun.

Up a narrow trail we raced, following the barely visible track of an ancient path that curved across the chaparral-covered slope. Around the base of a wind-carved, sandstone spire we charged, and then out of the corner of my eye, I caught the briefest glimpse of a figure lurking on a ledge.

The next instant, a knife flashed in front of my face and a forearm like a bar of iron struck me across the neck. Shawnee plunged, unbalanced, rearing and shaking herself, while I parted company with my saddle and lit with a crash in a patch of sage and greasewood.

Instinctively, both my hands closed around the wrist of the attacker's hand that held the knife. Over and over we rolled, fighting for possession of the blade, for what seemed like an eternity, before I ended on top and pressed the point downward toward my assailant's throat.

"Don't, Andrew!" Tor's voice shouted. "Let him up!"

The savage face panting a few inches beneath my own belonged to Alzado; so did the twelve-inch sharpened steel. "He tried to kill me!" I yelled back.

"Not so, neither! Look up on the trail — on the rock just ahead."

The snarling jaws of the great mountain lion parted in a scream of hatred and pain. He crouched in a crevice right beside where Shawnee's next few strides would have carried us if we had not been swept off the trail by Alzado's leap.

While my head was still spinning and my breath was coming in short jerks, Fowler took careful aim and fired. Even at the moment of his death, the mountain lion jumped straight outward at his pursuers . . . a defiant lunge of barred claws that carried him across twenty feet of space before he hit the ground, dead.

"That cat was crazy — more so than ever, since I wounded him and let him get away," Tor explained. "If Alzado hadn't jumped when he did, I don't know what mighta happened."

"Why didn't you yell or something?" I said.

"No time," Alzado gasped. "Then, no breath." He added, "Señor is hombre fuerte."

A strong man, he had called me, and I knew he was reliving just how close the point of the

113

knife had been to his throat.

"I'm sorry for the mistake," I said, stretching out my hand and pulling him to his feet. "And mighty in your debt, too."

Alzado shrugged. "It was nothing," he said.

"Nothing!" Tor snorted, raising the dead lion's head and pulling back the lips to expose two-inch-long fangs. "That wounded cat was ducking in and out of the brush and the boulders, an' Alzado was right behind him on the blood trail with nothing but that pigsticker in his hand."

"Where's your gun?" I asked him.

"I have none."

"Well, you do now," I said. I handed him the Allen. The barest hint of a smile wrinkled the corners of his mouth, and then it was back to business as usual. "Gracias," he said, and then, "I will skin the leon."

Shawnee's and Tor's mounts rolled their eyes and trotted a nervous distance away from Alzado's big bay. Even minus his insides, the cougar's rolled-up hide made a large bundle behind the Yaqui's saddle. We three rode in a jovial mood, congratulating ourselves on the success of our effort and discussing the cunning of the adversary. I also noted an occasional admiring glance downward by Alzado as he studied his new rifle. Each time I saw that look, it made me check my boot top where the bone hilt of a newly acquired Yaqui knife protruded.

By the swirling dust on the horizon, we knew that our line had been true and that we had almost reached the drive. It crossed my mind that there would be some new stories to tell around the cook fire this night, and perhaps the morale of all would get a boost.

Behind the mass of dark shapes that was the herd proper was a separate smaller bunch of animals that made up the remuda. Joaquin was driving the string of horses into a grassy hollow enclosed by willows for a noon rest. I nodded approvingly to myself, and directed our course that way.

I was looking again at the rolled-up lion skin and thinking how impressed Joaquin would be. As we rode over the rim of the small bowl, the horse herd appeared right below us. I saw Joaquin's small figure snatch something up off the ground and point it toward us. A puff of smoke clouded his face and something clipped a lock of Tor's hair. A second later the report of the rifle reached us.

I set Shawnee at a gallop and waved my arms while shouting, "Don't shoot! It's us! Joaquin, don't shoot!"

The warning was unnecessary. A cuff from Gomez caught Joaquin upside the head and knocked him sprawling. The vaquero grabbed the boy up again and shook him fiercely. "Stupid, stupid boy!" he yelled in Joaquin's face. "You almost killed Señor Fowler!"

Gomez had drawn back his fist to strike the boy again when I reined Shawnee to a halt of flashing hooves and flung myself off her back. "That's enough!" I ordered. "Joaquin, why did you shoot at us?"

Tears were streaming down the boy's cheeks, and his throat was too constricted to answer. "Señor Andrew, I . . . he —" He stopped, too choked to say more. Then he turned and ran off.

CHAPTER 12

The next several days slipped by without incident as we moved the herd through the mountains by way of Tejon Pass. The terrain was rough and progress slow. A cold wind blew in our faces, while above us the light of the sun was darkened by the migration of millions of wild geese and ducks. This served as a reminder that winter was just around the corner. We had to deliver the herd in the north before the first snow arrived or face being stranded for the winter in the valley.

Peter, James, and John Reed worked with the skill and grit I had seen demonstrated by the best Californio vaqueros. They made even the hardest work into sport. Each hour was filled with contests in riding and roping. When matching their skill against the other riders, the brothers worked together like three fingers on the same hand. Dozens of times each day I could hear their laughter echo across the herd. They were polite to others of our little band, but there was the strong bond of kinship that naturally excluded anyone else from entering their tight circle. The other vaqueros treated the Reed brothers with respect due to young princes in line to inherit a great kingdom. Alzado would not think twice about barking commands to Joaquin, yet he pressed his thin lips together and held his peace when Peter, James, or John rode by. Many times I noticed conversations would die away when the Reed brothers, Tor, or I would come within earshot. Often, furtive, uncomfortable looks would follow. At first I believed that this attitude was in deference to our authority, and then I began to wonder exactly what the vaqueros were speaking of that they did not wish for us to hear. Joaquin's behavior became silent and almost fearful in the presence of these men.

Perhaps it was the prospect of weeks of this slow and tedious journey that affected the riders, I reasoned. And then the laughter of the Reed brothers reminded me that some among us were enjoying the adventure. Why then did the vaqueros seem so resentful as we topped the rise and began our descent down into the great San Joaquin Valley of Central California? Why the hard looks boring into the backs of Tor and me? Why the reluctant nod when we gave the order for some common task? As I looked out over the enormous, cloud-filled valley below me, I could not help but wonder again if Will Reed had chosen these vaqueros wisely. Without families to return to on the rancho, what was to tie these men to the herd and the job before us? More than once I imagined I glimpsed the thought of mutiny in their eyes. Resentment seethed just below the surface and was put aside only when the fierce Alzado rode among them shouting orders.

The chill I felt was more than a change in the

weather. It seemed that I was not the only one to notice.

Cattle picked their way down the rocky slopes. Ten thousand feet above the herd, the din of a million honking geese covered the sound of bawling cows. I did not hear the approach of Tor's horse until he was beside me. Tor jerked a thumb skyward and shook his head as though he had water in his ears. He shouted to make himself heard above the roar.

"Don't look now, but somethin's up between Alzado and that smilin' sneak Gomez."

I started to look over my shoulder, but Tor stopped me with a shake of his head.

"I said don't look," he instructed. "Best pay 'em no mind. But they had some words. Came to blows in the saddle. Alzado knocked Gomez off his horse. There'll be blood spilt over it if I know anythin'."

"Been building toward it," I remarked, gazing out over the top of the clouds as if we were discussing the valley.

"The vaqueros don't seem overfond of Alzado, that's for certain. They're skeert of him. Maybe that ain't all bad. I'm a little skeert of him, too." He grinned sheepishly. "A right unusual feller. I don't trust him. But then I don't trust none of the rest of 'em neither. Mebbe they'll jest fight among themselves and leave us out of it."

"Don't mind that as long as we get the herd where it's going," I agreed.

Tor looked toward Joaquin, who was riding

alone on the far side of the herd. "The boy ain't said two words since the other day. Don't look nobody in the eye. Ducks and runs ever'time anybody comes near. What do you make of it, Andrew?"

"He feels foolish, I reckon."

Tor tugged his beard. "I got me a feelin' . . . mebbe somethin' else."

"You tried talking to him?"

"Don't do no good. You'd best keep yer eye peeled, Andrew. I got me a real feelin'. Trouble's on the wind. We're headed into foggy territory, and somethin' don't sit right here with that Alzado and Gomez and the rest of the mob."

"And Joaquin?"

"Keep 'im close, Andrew. My bones is a tellin' me that boy knows somethin' he wishes he didn't know. Mebbe it's somethin' to do with us and the herd, and mebbe it ain't. But it bears watchin'."

There was no use pretending I had not noticed the way Joaquin ate off by himself and rode alone and spoke no word to anyone. No use pretending I had not noticed his hands trembling when Alzado or Gomez rode by. Tor's warning was only a confirmation of the same uneasiness I had been feeling for days.

CHAPTER 13

The clacking of a thousand pair of long, curved horns resounded from the herd like the clash of sabres in battle. The cattle seemed to sense the broad, swift barrier of the river just ahead of us. They bawled and tossed their heads nervously as we drove them on.

The river was called Rio Bravo by the first Spanish explorers. The north and south fork came together high in the Sierras and then roared down from the mountain through a steep, rocky gorge to tumble out onto the valley floor. Since those early days, the Powerful River has been renamed Kern, as though it were as tame as a small brook. But the roar of its waters has been the last sound in the ears of many men. Even where the river appears peaceful, the placid flow conceals a treacherous undercurrent ripping just beneath the surface. Maybe the Spaniards called the river "Bravo" because it took a strong man to ford it. To the west, it became shallow as it emptied into the marshes of the valley floor. Mud bogs and mires of quicksand made it impossible for us to cross there. Indians told of whole herds of elk being trapped and dying in the swamps after following a buck that strayed only a few yards from the trail.

Instead of risking such danger, we skirted the southern rim of the valley, moving on high ground toward the mouth of the river canyon. The torrent exploded from this boulder-strewn funnel and then seemed to collect itself in quiet pools before it sighed and moved on. There was one possible fording place that Tor and I knew of. I had made the passage several times on Shawnee. With the water low, we had driven my small herd across it easily. But rains had swelled the waters since then. The river was a quarter mile wide now, and deep enough that it would have to be swum. It was one thing to wade across a shallow flow. This was another matter entirely. Above us to the east, the current was impassable. Below us to the west lay the quicksand. We scratched our heads and looked the situation over. Were we brave enough to face the river?

Alzado spurred his big bay gelding to the edge of the bank. He stared at the far shore for an instant, then, making the sign of the cross, he plunged ahead, whooping as the horse hit the water. Urged on by Alzado's shouts and the sting of a quirt on its butt, the horse cut through the water without looking back. Straight across he swam as Alzado held its mane and yipped like a coyote. Emerging on the opposite side of the flow, the soaking vaquero reined the horse around, stood in his stirrups, and raised his sombrero in victory. He cupped his hand around his mouth and called over to us. "She is nothing, Señor Andrew! Deep, yes. But slow and lazy!"

As if to prove his point, he again rode down the bank and spurred his animal into the river to swim back. Brave Alzado had matched the Bravo with apparent ease. He called the treacherous stream "a woman" and in his mocking smile dared us all to follow after.

I unsheathed my bullwhip as all others of our troop took positions at the sides and rear of the herd. Dog was called to jump onto the saddle with Joaquin. I turned to the boy, who seemed not so eager as the Reed brothers for this adventure.

"Stay right with me, Joaquin," I commanded. "Do you hear me, boy? No matter what happens, you keep your horse tight behind me."

Joaquin nodded curtly and wrapped his fingers in Dog's leather collar. "We will follow you, Señor Andrew," he replied grimly. "Me and Dog are not afraid."

I knew Joaquin was not much of a swimmer. He was not even much for taking a bath in a water trough, and we were in for quite a baptism here. The cattle bellowed their protest as we lassoed the horns of the leaders and whipped and whooped them into the river from all sides. They made a black, bobbing counter current, heads raised and horns tangled. The Reed boys brought up the rear. Alzado, Rodriguez, and Garcia took the high side of the current with me and Joaquin. I spotted Tor on the down side with the soft, frightened-looking Gomez close behind him. Sanchez and Ortiz followed after.

Icy water soaked my buckskins and filled my

123

boots. Popping my whip behind the ears of the reluctant steers kept their course straight. The first of the animals emerged on the northern shore, bawled and shook themselves, then trotted forward.

Alzado turned and plunged back into the water to keep the central core of the group moving. I started to follow him, but it was at that moment I noticed that Tor was in trouble. He had lassoed an enormous animal around the horns. The critter was foundering! Caught up in some undertow, the beast had rolled over and now was tangled in the reata. To my horror, I saw that the reata was also looped around Tor's saddle horn and somehow caught beneath his stirrup leather. He and his strong bay horse were being pulled downstream. Gomez, who was within a few yards of my friend, did not seem to notice, or if he saw Tor's predicament, he offered no assistance. I shouted and rode through the herd as the head of Tor's mount screwed around in a desperate attempt to struggle free. With no more than a nudge, Shawnee leapt from the embankment and swam toward Tor as though she knew the urgency. For an instant I saw Tor's hand raise up. Light glinted on the blade of his knife as he tried to cut his mount loose from the reata. And then suddenly Tor and his horse parted company. The horse righted itself and, after a moment of confusion, swam toward shore. I could plainly see that the cinch on the saddle had broken. Tor bobbed up once and then went under. The wayward steer paddled on, dragging the saddle after.

"Tor!" I shouted. Gomez paid no mind to the struggle of my drowning comrade. He urged his mount in a straight line toward dry land while Tor splashed and gasped and sank a second time from sight. The churning hooves of a thousand beeves swept past him. One blow would be enough to finish him off! Two more steers broke away to tumble downstream just ahead of me. Where was Tor? I cracked my whip, urging Shawnee onward, although she could swim no faster. The waters were murky brown. I could not see Tor. Had he been sucked beneath the cattle? Was he swept away?

"Gomez!" I cried as the vaquero passed me. "Get back! Tor has fallen." The Mexican seemed not to hear me.

Seconds dragged by. Too long for a man to be beneath the water without a breath! I called out to heaven for help! Was the life of Tor Fowler to end in such a way?

I spotted a fragment of red flannel just beneath the surface. "Tor!" I shouted, turning Shawnee toward the spark of color that gave me hope! Twenty feet from me the hand of Tor groped upward. Then his face emerged for one feeble breath before he rolled and sank out of my sight again. Fearful that Shawnee might strike him with a hoof, I leapt from her back without thinking. My bullwhip still coiled in my hand, I struck out to where I had seen the color. Diving beneath the surface, I reached through the water hoping to grasp him. Nothing! Another quick breath and then I went under again. This time, my fingers brushed his limp body. I grasped him by the belt and struggled to hold him up. Only now did my own desperate situation come to mind. Here I was, only a fair swimmer, holding an unconscious man in the middle of a river! My lungs ached for air! I surfaced, gasped, half-shouted with terror and joy at what I saw!

There was little Joaquin on his horse, only ten feet from us! He had obeyed my command to stick tight on my tail. Now he held Shawnee by the reins and cried out to me!

"Your whip! Señor Andrew!"

Catching his intent, I managed to toss out the lash. He caught hold of the tip and looped it around his horn.

I strengthened my hold on Tor and held fast to the whip handle as the boy towed us toward dry land. Only then did he release Shawnee, who cut a path through the water ahead of us.

I did not let go of the bullwhip or Tor until we were dragged twenty yards up the embankment. Cold and shaken, I lay in the sand until a circle of riders came around, and Dog whined and licked my face. Tor coughed and moaned and asked if he were dead.

We had survived, thanks to Joaquin. And no thanks to Gomez.

I stood slowly and looked at the boy. "What were you doing out there, Joaquin," I scowled. "Don't you know you could have been killed?"

"You said I should follow you, Señor Andrew," he replied. There was a renewed confidence in the boy. He had redeemed himself as well as Tor and me that day.

The herd milled aimlessly about on the north shore of the Rio Bravo, but Tor and I were too tired to care. I waved feebly for Joaquin. "Tell Peter to make camp here," I coughed. "This is as far as we go today." The boy scampered off, relief written on his face.

Tor retched and coughed up some river water. He was hugging a boulder with his face pressed against it. It was a gesture I understood. Things were still swirling some for me as well. "What happened, Andrew?" he said.

"Your cinch busted," I said. "It's a good thing Joaquin took me so at my word, or you and I would both have been in trouble, pard."

Dragging himself upright, Tor stood swaying unhappily and frowning. "What's your all-fired hurry?" I wanted to know.

"Got a problem," he said quietly. "That cinch was new."

While all the men were shaking out their belongings to dry, Fowler and I had an inconspicuous meeting with Peter Reed. The eldest brother had caught up with the wayward steer still dragging Tor's reata and the waterlogged saddle.

Fowler looked with disgust at the battered leather. "Tore it up . . . just flat tore it up. But looky here."

He was right. The horsehair girth was still intact, the metal buckle ring shining. Not a single strand had parted. Tor ran his hand upward to the leather

127

strap that secured the girth to the saddle. "Now look at this."

Peter and I saw where the leather had ripped across when the weight of the steer and the force of tons of water had pulled against the reata. Fowler flipped the strap over in his hand. There, on the back and at a place that would have been out of sight up under the skirt of the saddle was the faint but still perceptible mark of a knife. "This didn't happen of its own self," Tor growled. "Somebody give it a good start and then waited for somethin' to happen."

"But who?" Peter wondered aloud. "Who would have done such a thing?"

"And when was it done?" I added. "There's no way to tell from this."

"What should we do?" was Peter's next question.

"Here's my thinking on it," Tor said. "Some low-down snake has took great pains to see to it that this looked like a accident. Let's just let him go on a thinkin' thataway."

I studied the roiling waters that had so nearly cost two lives, then looked again at the knife mark. "You're right," I agreed at last. "Let's play this close and see who tries to up the ante next."

"Shall I tell my brothers, or Joaquin?" Peter wanted to know.

"No," I said. "The less who know we're on to it, the smaller the chance of giving the game away. We have to keep this just between us three." It was to prove a fatal mistake.

CHAPTER 14

Sunlight broke through the morning haze and warmed our backs as we rode on. Lizards awoke and slithered out onto boulders and fallen logs to soak up the last bit of sun before winter closed in.

The feel of Indian summer might have warmed my spirits as well, but there was a chill in my soul that had nothing to do with temperature. I found myself studying each man among us, mentally calculating what motive there might be for attempting to murder Tor. Why stage an accident when a knife between the ribs in the dark night would accomplish the same purpose? I doubted each man in turn and then all of them together. After a time I talked myself into doubting my doubts. Perhaps the cinch had been cut halfway through long before we ever left on the drive. Maybe our vaqueros had nothing to do with it. Wasn't it possible that the leather cinch had been scored by some disgruntled enemy back in Angel's Camp? The man who had done the deed was certainly patient if that was the case. He had been counting on the fact that one day there would be just enough strain on the leather that it would snap at a crucial moment and take Tor with it.

"You're payin' more mind to the hired help than the cattle," Tor commented, riding up beside me. His gaze followed mine to Alzado as the Indian shouted and cursed a wayward steer.

"I expect you're right," I agreed. I had not been thinking much about business. "Trying to figure who it is. Or if it's all of them. Or maybe none of them. Maybe this is an old score," I said hopefully.

"Ain't all of 'em." Tor kept his eyes on Alzado and then scanned the other vaqueros who rode in pairs and singly all around us. "But it's some of 'em."

"How can you know that?"

" 'Cause if it was the bunch of 'em what wanted us dead, there wouldn't be much to stop 'em. They'd of stuck us to the ground while we was sleepin' if they had a mind to. No sir, Andrew, it ain't all of 'em. Mebbe most of 'em is in on this, but there's some of 'em who ain't. Elsewise they wouldn't wait to make a move." He drew a finger across his throat to make his point. "If they aim to rustle the cattle and kill us all at once, I reckon they'll wait till we're closer to the gold fields. After all, we're still some use for drivin'. Takes lots of men to move a herd like this. They won't want us all dead till they see the end of the trail."

"You figure they aim to steal the herd?"

"Can't figger no other reason why they'd want to pick us off one by one."

"You ought to feel real proud, Tor." I tried

130

to make light of our predicament. "They tried to kill you first. I guess that means they're most scared of you."

He did not smile, but looked across the mass of swaying critters. "It's a matter of cuttin' the wolves out of the pack, Andrew. We got to be mighty careful about now. Don't want to bring down the good 'uns with the rotten apples, if you take my meanin'."

"I can't tell the good ones from the spoilt ones," I said. "And that's what's got me bothered."

We both looked at Alzado at the same instant. There was something menacing in the manner of the Yaqui. His face was a scowl set in leather and stone. He was feared by the others; hated by Gomez.

I opened my mouth to speak, thought better of it, and then blurted out my thought, "He could have let that lion kill me. Saved himself the trouble. That would have been one less of us to do in."

Tor nodded thoughtfully. "I been figgerin' on that one too, Andrew. Don't make no sense . . . except . . . we was only a day's ride from the Reed Rancho. If you'd been kilt, we would have turned back for sure. Taken the herd right back to the rancho. Nope. If Alzado is leader of the pack of wolves, he's thinkin' like a wolf, too. Draw the prey away from the main herd. See? Here we are a hunert miles from Will Reed and his help. You, me, Peter, and three boys. It won't take much when they figger we ain't a use to 'em no more."

I frowned and narrowed my eyes as Alzado

whooped and whipped his mount to a gallop to head off another stray. Tor's reasoning made sense. And there was that warning from Gomez that Alzado kept company with bandidos. But what about Gomez? I trusted the groveling little snake even less than I trusted Alzado. "You said that Gomez and Alzado got into it the other day?"

"I don't trust neither of them two," Tor muttered. "They wasn't arguing about how to throw a loop, I'll wager. More likely they was fightin' over when to throw it and whose neck they was goin' to throw it around, if you folla me." He rubbed his neck in a nervous gesture, as though he had already imagined his neck in a noose.

"You think there are any others besides those two?"

"Them two for sure. Well, I'm almost sure. As for the rest of 'em . . . I don't know. I just figger I ain't gonna be sleepin' none too sound till we get these critters checked into somebody else's corral." He shook his head. "A new kind of claim jumper. Here in the valley there ain't no law to stop 'em, neither." He patted the stock of his rifle. "Jest this kind of law. And I'm keepin' her loaded and ready, too." Now he smiled reproachfully at me. " 'Course you gave your Allen rifle to our friend Alzado, didn't you? Love your enemy, Andrew, but don't give 'im your rifle, I always say."

Tor did not have to remind me of my foolish gesture of gratitude. A dozen times that afternoon I found myself regretting that I had traded my rifle for Alzado's knife. I looked down at the smooth antler handle of the weapon protruding from my boot top, and then I looked at the stock of the Allen in its sheath on Alzado's saddle. I could not help but wonder now if my old Allen might soon be used against me.

CHAPTER 15

We were camped along a nameless creek that wandered down from the high Sierras. The Reed brothers stood first watch while the rest of us gathered in close to the fire and tried to get some sleep after a supper of bacon and beans.

There was not much conversation. These men were mostly strays. Lonesome critters without home or family, they worked on one rancho and then another, never staying long in any set place. Sometimes their pasts found common ground. Garcia and Sanchez talked softly about a cantina girl named Rosa from down Sonora way. The two men had never met each other before coming to the Reed rancho, but both had loved Rosa. Both had gotten drunk in that cantina. Both had been beaten and robbed. Could their beloved Rosa have been a part of the plot? This common betrayal somehow made them brothers. They cast around in their memories to compare what other places they might have in common. Nothing. Only Rosa and the Sonora cantina. It was enough for a long conversation. I fell asleep listening to their soft laughter and the crackle of the fire.

When I awoke, all was silent. The blaze had died to embers, and I judged it to be another hour before my watch began. Another hour to sleep, I thought, snuggling deeper into my blanket. I opened one eye and looked at the orange coals. If I stayed put, the fire would die before Tor's watch was up, and we'd all sleep cold and have cold breakfast in the morning. There was a small heap of dry sticks outside our circle. I hoped that someone else would wake up and stoke the fire, but no one seemed to notice the chill but me.

I pulled my blanket around me and sat up slowly. My boots were drying next to the fire. I picked up the right one, shook it out and slipped it over my bare foot. Standing, I started to put on my left boot as well. My fingers grasped the upper leather and my toes were just above the opening when I felt the tanned hide tremble and caught a glimpse of something moving — slithering — inside my boot. I gasped, tossed the thing away from me just as the air was filled with a bright buzzing sound like bacon frying.

"Rattler!" I cried, stumbling back as the creature spilled from my boot and coiled on top of it. I had not fallen back far enough. The snake fixed its black, evil eyes on my outstretched leg. It buzzed afresh, and every man in the camp lay stock-still and watching.

From across the fire pit Peter Reed whispered in a hoarse voice. "Don't move, Señor Andrew. No one move."

Don't move? I wanted to holler and run for a mile. Yet less than a yard from my big toe that rattler held me prisoner. I dared not speak and

135

held my breath as I watched Peter's shadowed form reach cautiously for his rifle.

Even as I lay there, I knew for certain that the deadly creature had not gotten into my boot without help from some two-legged snake in the camp. I was not supposed to find it until a set of fangs pierced my foot. Even if I had shaken it out, it would have landed right next to me.

Peter stood slowly and raised his weapon to his shoulder. If he did not split the head of the thing with the first shot, I was still a dead man. Even wounded it would strike me.

The hammer clicked back. Every sound was a threat to the rattler. It moved its flat, hideous head from side to side as if to see which part of my flesh was best to bite. The buzz of its rattles quickened until the air was full of the warning.

All around me I could see the firelight glinting in the eyes of the silent spectators watching me. Which one of them had planned this little performance? Whoever he was, his intent was more vile than that of the snake that faced me now.

"Peter . . ." James Reed muttered his brother's name fearfully.

Beads of perspiration stood out on my forehead and trickled into my eyes. In an instant I expected to feel the fire of fangs ripping into me. Drawing a slow breath, I silently prayed that the aim of Peter Reed would be true. The young man's eyes narrowed as he stared at the back of the swaying dark head of the viper. His muscles tensed, and then the air exploded with fire and smoke. The head of the rattler tore away and flew past my face. Its jaws opened and closed as though to strike even though separated from the writhing body. The headless thing flipped and fell across my legs. I shouted and grasped at it, tossing it into the fire where it still struggled in death amid the embers.

Alzado leapt to his feet and, grabbing up a stick, rescued the body of the snake from the heat. He laid it belly up on a rock, cut off the rattles, and tossed them to me like a prize.

"Twelve buttons," Alzado said. There was a hint of a smile on his leathery face. He was plainly amused by what had happened. "Keep it for luck."

I was about to say that I needed all the luck I could get when Peter stepped forward. He swept his rifle around at each smiling vaquero until their smirks disappeared. It was his way of saying that he would blow the head off of any human snake if the need arose. The men shrugged or looked away uncomfortably, as though to say they understood.

Alzado skinned the snake and fried the white meat. I did not eat any, but I tied the twelve-button rattle around my neck by a leather string as a reminder that the real snake among us was still alive.

"Wake up, Andrew!" Tor shook me awake, and believe me, after the experience with the snake, it did not take much.

"What is it?"

"Rodriguez is gone!"

"Gone? What do you mean, gone?"

"Made off with the palomino horse that Gomez rides. Prob'ly the fastest mount here, savin' yore Shawnee, of course."

"Are you certain he's not around somewhere?"

"Positive. He was s'posed to be the guard that I relieved for the last watch. When I got out there, he was already gone. Well, I just figgered he slipped into camp a little early or I'd missed him on the other side of the drove, but the others say he didn't come back atall."

I eyed my boots with renewed curiosity and touched the rattles tied around my neck. "Do you think that means he's been the one trying to cross us up?"

Tor considered this notion, then said, "Possible, or maybe that's what we're s'posed to think so as to make us let down our guard. Or mayhap he was a good'un run off by fear of the others. Naw, Andrew, I reckon we don't know much more than we did, 'ceptin' now we're short one hand and one powerful fast horse."

Not for the first time I wondered if we needed some help. "Maybe you should ride on ahead and fetch Ames with some more hands," I suggested. "Maybe Rodriguez works for Powers."

Fowler shushed me with a look and jerked his chin to the side. There, casually coiling a lariat, but well within earshot, was the brooding figure of Alzado.

CHAPTER 16

The light in Peter Reed's green eyes danced in the reflected glitter of the stream called Mariposas. The fall air was full of a drifting cloud of orange and black wings.

"Butterflies," he said. A grin marched across his freckled features. "That's the stream's name. My grandfather told me that the old Spanish explorers had never seen so many butterflies as in the meadows on the banks of this place."

"It is an amazing sight," I agreed. "And for those pious men to leave off using the names of saints when they went to make note of this river says that they were very impressed indeed."

We were long past the near calamity and only a few days travel from our destination. The spirit of high adventure with which the Reed brothers had begun the drive had reasserted itself.

"Thank you, Señor Andrew," Peter said, "for bringing me. I have often imagined this spot, but never knew when I might get to see it."

The stream of water curved around a little oak-topped knoll. The herd settled in to feed on a rich, grassy meadow, while we made our camp on top of the rise. Thousands of butterflies floated into the grove of trees until they clustered on the trunks like heavy drapery. Peter and I stood and watched as the sun went down and the men gathered for supper.

The vaqueros sat apart and talked among themselves. Tor kept the Reed boys and Joaquin spellbound with his tall tales of life in the mountains. He told them the story of how he had experienced an especially difficult time saddling an uncooperative mule on one extremely foggy night, only to have daylight reveal that he was riding a grizzly bear. I think Joaquin and John, the youngest Reed, believed him.

Our discussion came round to the boys' future plans. Joaquin was excited to learn that John would be returning to school in the Kingdom of Hawaii. After just one month in the island kingdom, John assured Joaquin, he would swim like a dolphin and glide his canoe over the sea like a flying fish.

James, the middle brother, would be entering Harvard to study law. "Father says that now that California belongs to the United States, we must have at least one in the family who knows Yankee law, and I'm elected."

I turned to Peter, who was watching his brothers with some amusement and yet, I thought, a touch of sadness. "What are your plans, Peter?"

The young man took a deep breath. Before replying, he brushed a hunk of dark red hair back off his forehead. "Father says I am to go to the States with James. He says we need more Yankee business sense." Peter sighed heavily.

"And you ain't happy to be goin'?" Tor asked.

"Where'd you druther go?"

"Go?" Peter said. "I don't want to leave at all. I love California. It has everything — the seashore, the high mountains, the herds and the rodeos, the places still waiting to be explored. . . . If I live to be a hundred, I could never see it all. I'll go to please Father, but I'll be back to stay."

He stood up and unfolded the heavy leather chapederos on which he had been sitting. Peter buckled them on, readying himself to take his turn as night herder when Alzado and Sanchez came in.

The Yaqui arrived just as Peter returned from saddling his curly-coated horse. As they entered the circle of firelight, I noticed that the animal was limping.

"Hold on, Peter," I said. "Chino is favoring his near hind hoof."

A quick examination showed no obvious injury, but it was plain that the horse would see no duty that night. Peter started to lead Chino back to the remuda in order to select another mount when Alzado stopped him. "Take my horse, Don Peter," the Yaqui offered. "We have only walked a little, and he is still fresh."

"Gracias, Alzado. Shall we swap the saddles?"

"No importante. You are of a height with me. Just take him, if you wish."

It was a couple hours later that the wind came up out of the east. The fire had died down and everyone was asleep, except Peter and the other night herder, Gomez. As near as I could later figure, Peter had posted himself on Alzado's bay at the north end of the herd. It was a place where the oaks from the knoll trooped down to drink with the willows.

The Santa Ana winds blow up out of the eastern deserts of California. They whistle through the mountain passes and down the western slopes, sometimes blowing dust in mile-high clouds. The east wind always makes people and critters restless. Sailors look to their anchor rodes, and herds stir and mill about. Most times the wind dies down after a while, and the unease passes.

This one came up all of a sudden. From perfect stillness, the night changed to high streaky clouds racing overhead. Clumps of butterflies were ripped off the tree bark. They bumbled in confusion across the pitch-black meadow, colliding with the noses of startled cows.

For all that, there was no great cause for alarm. The herd had done twenty miles that day. They were tired, well fed, and would not be easily roused. A little quiet talking or singing and they would have quieted right down. I know this is true, and have thought it over many times through the years.

It was the gunshot that ended all hope of calling things back. Somewhere around the south end of the drove, a rifle exploded. Besides the shattering noise, the flash was like a lightning strike in its brilliance.

How can I picture the awful dread with which a stampede is regarded? I could compare it to an avalanche, to a runaway steam locomotive, or to an earthquake and a tornado rolled into one, but no description is really adequate.

The vaqueros awoke with a rumble that they felt in their souls even before the bellowing roars had penetrated their sleep-muffled hearing. "El ganado! El ganado!" they cried. "The cattle!" At that moment, the expression no longer called to mind a placid, cud-chewing band of stupid animals. From a drowsy jumble of fitful complaints, the herd was transformed into a single beast with four thousand legs and two thousand tossing horns, but only a single thought — to get far away from that terrible blast as quickly and as directly as possible.

At that moment, any plan to reach a horse and head off the charging mass of beef was discarded in the same second that it entered the mind. The only idea of any interest was to save oneself any way at all.

I struggled free of the ground sheet in which I was wrapped and saw Joaquin nearby still wrestling to get out of his bedroll. I picked him up, canvas covering and all, tossed him toward the branch of an oak and yelled, "Climb!"

By the flickers of the dying embers, I saw Tor do the same with John Reed. My attention changed then to the hundred or so head of cows that seemed to be headed directly for me. Individual hooves could not be heard, not the bawling of separate throats. All sound massed together in a noise so fearful that one felt overrun and trampled even before the first wave of steers reached the little knoll.

Dodging the fastest of the wild-eyed critters drove me away from the trees that had branches close to the ground. I found myself beside an immense water oak of perhaps sixty-foot height and twenty of girth. It gave me protection from the initial rush, but like a wave that rolls both up and back the beach, a stampede carries away all imagined places of safety that it touches.

Over my head, but higher than I could jump, a large snag of a limb jutted out. I always sleep with my coiled blacksnake whip close to hand, and as on other occasions, this habit saved my life. A flick upward looped the whip around the limb, and I shinnied up as I have never climbed before. The spiked tip of a angrily pitching horn gored the calf of my leg, but then I was up and out of harm's way.

From my perch I looked out over a floodtide of steers that trampled bedrolls, belongings, and even the remains of the fire. Smaller trees shuddered and collapsed under the onslaught, and the larger ones resounded from the repeated collisions until it was all one could do to hang on.

Across the meadow, over by the stream, the moonlight reflected off the water. Silhouetted against that patch of silver illumination, I saw Peter Reed on the bay horse. He was urging his mount in twisting and corkscrewing, trying to move with the flow of a new peril as he was carried along the creek, but it seemed that he would win free to the far side of the water. Up the steep bank should be safety.

I saw the bay rear and plunge, once and then again. I saw Peter's shadow rocking with the jolts of the bucking ride. Then the shapes merged with the great beast called stampede, and I could not see either the horse or the rider anymore.

When the rush had passed, we climbed down from our perches and out of whatever other crevices had presented themselves as refuges. In the head count around the remains of our camp, all were accounted for except Peter. By some miracle, there were no serious injuries. The hole poked in my leg was typical. There were cuts and bruises in plenty, but no broken bones. Being camped on the little hill had saved us, I guess. It had slowed down the charge enough for each of us to find a place of safety.

John cried and begged for us to go looking for Peter. I whispered to Tor what I had seen, and then we told the boys to stay and pick up what they could salvage of the supplies while the adults searched.

Dog was missing, too. Every minute or so, Joaquin would whistle and call for him, but he was nowhere around.

Just before we set out on foot, I saw Tor having words with Gomez. The vaquero was the only one of us still mounted, all the other horses having been run off by the stampede. I could not hear what was said, but I saw Gomez waving his arms, then pointing at the sky, the vanished herd of cattle, his horse, and lastly his rifle. When Fowler rejoined me, he made no comment, but shook his head with grim disgust. Tor and I concentrated on the area closest to where I had caught my last glimpse of Peter. There was a chance that he had gotten into the lee of a downed log or crawled in a hole. Perhaps he was injured or unconscious, but alive somewhere.

Even carrying blazing pine knots as torches, we found nothing until almost dawn. We had walked much farther along the stream than I thought was reasonable, but we did not want to turn back while any hope remained. How could we face the boys without knowing?

It was the bay horse that we came to first. Turned broadside to the force of the stampede, the bay had been carried along the creek like a twig on the crest of a flood. The saddle was missing.

A whine reached our ears from just west of the stream. Tor and I broke into a stumbling run. Around the next bend, half hidden by a clump of elderberries up on the bank, we came upon Dog. He acknowledged us with another whine, but did not come to greet us. He sat very still, his head cocked to one side. One forepaw rested on the lifeless body of Peter Reed.

Rolled up and tied over Tor's shoulder was the largest remaining fragment of his bedroll. After standing a moment in painful silence, we spread out the tarp and wrapped the young man's form to carry back to camp. "Come along, Dog," I said. Dog remained by a mound of earth near where he had found Peter. "Come on," I insisted. "What's the matter with you?"

Dog whined and began to dig into the mound. By the time I looked to see what he was seeking, he had uncovered what was left of Alzado's saddle. The thin light of the Sierra morning answered my question right off: The cinch leather had been cut part way through, high up and out of sight.

CHAPTER 17

Murder had been done to Peter Reed and murder was in my heart for the man who killed him. I slung the scored leather cinch strap over my shoulder to use as evidence in the trial of Alzado. Yet I had determined already that there would be no court, no judge, no jury in this case. I would kill him myself and with the same cold-bloodedness he had shown toward young Peter Reed.

Dog trotted alongside as we carried Peter's body back toward camp. Neither Tor nor I spoke for a long while. My thoughts flew to Francesca and Will Reed. All the gold in California could not buy them back their firstborn son! Nineteen years of love and hopes now lay trampled — wrapped in a tarp and slung between us like an empty sack. Will had trusted us with his sons. Francesca's fears had proved right. Three brothers had left home, and now only two would be returning. The sense of my own failure filled me like bitter gall. Alzado would pay for this grief with his own life, I determined. Tor had come to the same conclusion.

"Alzado," Tor muttered, "lamed the boy's horse and scored the cinch. Same as he done mine afore the river crossin'. Put that there rattler in your boot. Peter shot the wrong snake."

148

I nodded, but did not reply. Words failed me as we topped the rise and looked down on the little knoll where James and John Reed waited for news of their brother. They stood side by side, off a ways from the vaqueros and Joaquin. Their backs were toward us. Looking southward, no doubt their thoughts had also turned toward home — to Francesca and Will. I dreaded the moment when they would look back and see the burden we carried with us.

"Gomez!" spat Tor. "Fit for hangin' right along with Alzado. Dropped his gun, he says. Fired off accidental, he says. Spooked the herd. An accident, he says. Well, I say he was in on it with Alzado. Murder. The boy woulda made it if this cinch hadn't been cut. No jury gonna see it otherwise."

Below us, the men were standing, kneeling, or sitting in a tight circle. I counted only five men. Gomez, who had been the only one of us left with a horse, seemed to be missing. Had he ridden off like Rodriguez?

"Whoa up there, Andrew," Tor said, and we stopped for a better look. Lowering the body to the ground, we ducked behind a heap of boulders to reconnoiter what we now felt was an enemy camp. "There's Joaquin." The boy sat alone and forlorn on a fallen log. "The Reed boys . . ." Tor frowned. "I count only five vaqueros."

For a few seconds I studied the forms of the men below us. Hats, the slope of shoulders, shirts, and shapes told us that all were present on the hill but one. . . . "Alzado is gone," I said.

149

"So's that big chestnut Gomez was riding," Tor added. "Our pigeon has flown the coop."

When his oilcloth coat gaped open, it was easy to spot Gomez's bright yellow shirt from among the others. The center of attention, he was sitting on the ground and cradling a blood-stained arm.

"Alzado," I said as hate boiled up in me. "He's stolen Gomez's horse."

"That'll mean he got away with the only rifle that ain't been trampled. Gone to fetch his gang, unless I miss my guess."

If Gomez was part of the conspiracy, why had he been left behind? The framework of facts left much unexplained. Bullwhip on my belt and knife in my boot, I once again hefted Peter's body, and we started the descent into our shattered camp.

It was Joaquin who first spotted our coming. He raised his arm and shouted. James and John spun around to look, ran a few steps, then froze in the horror of what they saw. Making the sign of the cross, they sank to their knees.

Leaving the wounded Gomez on the knoll, Sanchez, Garcia, Ramos, and Ortiz ran to meet us. All four vaqueros were babbling at once.

"Alzado the Yaqui!"

"He and Gomez —"

"They argue —"

"Alzado pulls a knife!"

"He stabs poor Gomez —"

"He steals Gomez's horse!"

"Alzado is gone, Señor Andrew!"

Ramos and Ortiz offered to carry Peter, but we

did not relinquish the body until we reached the knoll. We placed the boy beneath the shade of an oak tree. Joaquin brought a blanket to cover the blood-soaked shroud as James and John held tightly to each other and staggered to Peter's side.

Gomez shouted at me, "I tell you, Señor Andrew." He bellowed and cradled his wounded arm. "I warn you that Alzado is a very bad man! You did not listen to me! I gave you warning!"

Tor whirled on the whimpering toady. "Shut up, Gomez! You ain't in the clear in this affair, neither!"

Gomez puckered his mouth like a petulant child and looked mournfully down at his arm. "You do not see I am wounded? Alzado has stolen my horse — no doubt to ride for bandidos who will kill us all and steal the herd!"

Impatient with these cries, Tor snatched the cinch from my shoulder and strode toward Gomez. Grabbing the vaquero up by his shirt front, he waved the severed leather under his nose. "What do you know about this?"

"Nothing!" cried Gomez in terror. The other vaqueros stepped back, exchanging fearful looks.

"Nothing?" Tor shook him like a rag doll. "The leather cut nearly clean through. Just like mine was at the river. And it was your gun what started the stampede!"

"An accident! I swear, señor! I dropped my gun! It was an accident! No, señor! It is Alzado who is the bandido! Alzado who has done this evil thing! I have nothing to do with Alzado! You see . . ."

151

He waved his bloody arm like a flag of surrender. "He tells me to get off my horse. He says he is leaving! I fight him, and he stabs me and steals my horse! I am left here wounded! Nearly killed! Can you not see, señor?" he begged. "I have done nothing wrong. I only tried to warn you. . . ."

James Reed looked up from the body of his brother. "It happened the way Gomez is telling it," James managed to speak. "No explanation from Alzado. At first I thought he was going to ride after the remuda. But he rode out of here hell-for-leather, and he didn't come back. Like Gomez told it."

Tor scowled down into the terrified face of Gomez, and then gave him one more shake, sending him sprawling back on the ground. I heard Tor mutter in a menacing voice, "Mebbe it's so and mebbe it ain't, you little worm. Fact is, 'twas your gun what started the stampede. I'll get back to that later."

James looked hard at the cinch and then at the covered remains of Peter. "Ah, Peter," he choked. "What will I say to Mother? What will I tell Father?"

With Alzado gone, fled on Gomez's horse, we were completely without mounts. That thought alone was enough to rekindle the flame of hatred I felt for the treacherous Yaqui. How were we to begin recovering from the disaster of the stampede and Peter's tragic death? Regardless of what else we may have sensed, the answer in practical terms was "on foot."

I dispatched the vaqueros to search for our horses. Things would level out some once we were remounted, but there was no telling how far the animals might have run in the terror of the night. Gomez started to whine about how his arm was hurting him, but I gave him no slack on that account. I knew the wound to be minor, no matter his complaints, and sent him out with the rest.

What came next was harder still. James and John were gathered around the canvas containing the body of their brother. Joaquin stood awkwardly by, unable to speak but unwilling to leave his friends. James looked up at my approach.

"The first three horses we recover are yours," I said. "No matter whose they are, they are yours to take Peter back home. I'll send one of the vaqueros along, or Tor." Fowler nodded his agreement.

"Take Peter home," James repeated hollowly. "Yes, we need to do that. He'll be buried next to Grandfather."

"I'm more sorry than I can say, boys. Peter was just telling me yesterday how glad he was to be here, but I wish now we had turned back at the first sign of trouble."

John sniffed. "When I got scared and wanted to go home, Peter told me not to be a baby. He said being a quitter would shame Father. Peter would never have left without finishing the drive."

"Well," I said simply, "we can't always control how things turn out. If it wasn't that I need to see to saving the rest of the herd for your father,

153

I'd throw in the hand now, too."

"No!" James said sharply. "We're not throwing in this hand!"

"Now, James," I began, "nobody expects —"

"No!" he said again, cutting me off. "We are here in Father's place, and I'm the oldest now, so I decide. I say our job is helping with the herd and catching up to Alzado. Father would be disappointed with anything less."

"But, boys, what about Peter? And your parents need to be told."

James shook his head decisively. "What's done can't be changed, so our folks don't have to hear about Peter till they also hear that we did what was needed. Besides, Peter liked this spot. It's a good enough resting place for now."

Tor, James, and I fashioned crude shovels from tree branches. We dug into a sandy space in the south side of the hill that was overhung by an earthen bank. Joaquin and John found two straight sticks, and these they bound together in the form of a cross by using leather strips salvaged from the remnants of busted reins.

We arranged Peter Reed's body in the cutout under the overhang and rolled up some rocks with which to cover the spot. When all was ready, James hesitated when his little brother said, "I don't know, James. We don't have a priest. What if this isn't holy ground?"

James looked around at the sky and the giant, patient oaks, then listened for a moment to the scolding call of a bluejay. "This is right," he said.

"God is here, even if a priest isn't."

Slanting beams of sunlight brightened the hill-side as we dug into the bank, collapsing it over the grave. We rolled the granite rocks atop the place, and when it was neat, John and Joaquin set up the cross. "Now," James said, "where do we begin tracking Alzado?"

CHAPTER 18

James was right. We could not linger around Peter Reed's grave. Already it was time to think of finding the horses and the herd. Attending to business, so to speak.

Folks fresh from the States or other civilized countries often believe that we of the West are short of a normal set of human emotions. We are described as unfeeling by those with more sheltered lives.

Let me record that such a charge is a slanderous lie. Unless a westerner is a hardened criminal or has abused liquor, he has no lack of feelings. Nor have our sensibilities been blunted. It is necessity that drives us to set aside emotions and press on.

I put the boys to work collecting all the remnants of provision and tack. Now every morsel of jerked beef and every scrap of bridle was precious.

Tor and I cobbled together pieces of reins and strips of leather cut from trampled saddles. We were making jaquimas, bridlepieces, which the gringos call hackamores, that would work without bits by pressure on the horses' noses and jaws.

Around noon the vaqueros returned, having located neither mounts nor steers. They were a footsore lot — walking far in high-heeled, pointed-toed boots was never done for pleasure.

I watched Gomez flop down with his back against an oak. So that he could sit without his pistol grip pressing into his gut, he pulled it from his belt and laid it beside him.

Gomez called Joaquin to him. The boy had recovered a stuff sack full of jerky and was distributing the dried meat to the men. The vaquero gestured for the boy to come closer, then spoke something to him. I saw Joaquin's limbs grow stiff and his spine turn rigid, as if he was hearing something that terrified him.

I wanted to go immediately and find out what was up, but decided to speak to the boy privately first. I poked idly about in the dirt, as if I were recovering something of use. To my surprise, there in the dust were two small fragments of Bible pages. My copy of the Good Book, which had traveled with me for more years than I could recall, now was torn to shreds and scattered. I stuffed the fragments of paper into my pocket without looking at them.

After Joaquin completed his rounds to all the vaqueros, I joined him near the fire. "What did he say to you?" I asked.

"Who, Señor Andrew?" He spoke as if he did not take my meaning, but his eyes flickered toward where Gomez lay.

"What are you afraid of, Joaquin? What did he say to you?"

Again his frame stiffened, and he glanced quickly at the vaquero who was toying idly with his pistol.

The bandaged knife wound did not seem to be causing Gomez any great distress.

"He said that we must hurry to find the horses. He says that Alzado has most certainly gone for the rest of Jack Powers' gang, and they will be returning to kill us and steal the herd."

I listened to the last sentence as I was already walking away from Joaquin over to Gomez's relaxed form. "Gomez," I called out, "what do you know of Powers? What are you hiding?"

"I? I am not hiding anything, señor," he said innocently. "I have heard it said that Alzado, the cursed savage, belongs to an outlaw band whose leader is the American Powers. If it is true, señor, it will mean much trouble for us."

Settled some by this explanation, I demanded, "But why frighten the boy? Why didn't you tell me directly?"

Gomez shrugged. "It is only hearsay, señor. I was just telling the muchacho of the great need to hurry and locate the horses. Perhaps he is easily frightened because of the stampede."

I reached down and grasped Gomez by the arm. I will admit that I took hold of the wrist on the wounded side on purpose. With one yank I stood the vaquero upright, spilling his pistol from his lap and his jerky into the dirt.

"You're exactly right about the need to hurry," I said. "Bring your food. You and I will go search together, and you can tell me all you know or have heard."

Gomez could not very well refuse a direct order

from the boss, no matter how tired he was. He made a great show of wincing when he touched his injured arm, but he tramped along out of the camp by my side. I whistled for Dog to join us, and we three set out. I carried one of our improvised bridles and Gomez carried another.

Once unleashed, Gomez's tongue babbled like the stream beside which we hiked. "There is much I know of Alzado, señor, but much more that is spoken of Jack Powers around the cantinas of the City of the Queen of the Angels, Los Angeles. Powers has used his skill at cards to gain enough money to hire some very bad men. It is said that he will soon rule the gold camps, far from any law that could touch him."

I nodded grimly at the remembrance of how Jack Powers had made himself out to be the law. "Go on," I said.

"This Powers has men who rob and kill along El Camino Real. He has those in the cantinas who report of who has much gold, and soon —" Gomez drew his thumb across his neck and made throat-cutting noises.

"And Alzado?" I asked. "Why an Indian vaquero?"

Gomez looked around as if he expected to see the Yaqui lurking behind a tree. "Powers is very clever. He knows he must have fresh horses with which his malditos may flee their crimes. On each rancho of renown, he keeps those who will steal the best mounts."

I looked down at the knife hilt showing above

my boot top. To think of the cutthroat Yaqui around Will and Francesca's home made me shudder . . . almost as bad as the thought of how far he had ridden with me unaware of his nature.

Dog had been ranging along on either side of us as we hiked. At my command he would explore branching side canyons and dive into thickets. He had on this occasion been out of sight long enough, and I whistled for him to return.

Imagine my delight when instead of Dog's recall, my signal was acknowledged by a bugle from Shawnee. Through the manzanita she came, sorrel and white flashing, leading a band of six horses with her.

Her tail was flagged, and she was obviously proud of herself. "So that's what kept you," I said, rubbing her nose. "You stopped to gather your friends."

My paint mare willingly accepted the unfamiliar bridle, while Gomez had somewhat more difficulty with his mount. "Drive these others back to camp," I said as the vaquero finished wrestling with the jaquima. "I'll have another look round for the cattle."

But where had Dog gotten off to? With Shawnee beneath me again, even though we were minus a saddle, things felt a lot better. I pointed Shawnee straight up the highest hill I could see close by in order to survey the countryside.

When we reached shale rock, we wound around the cone-shaped peak, spiraling upward till we emerged above the tree line. There below us was spread the terrain of the Sierras, like a map in a geography book. Looking south I could see the little knoll where we had camped and where Peter Reed now lay buried.

My eyes traced the wandering path of the creek to the point where Tor and I had discovered Peter's body, and still farther to where I had met up with Shawnee. I probed beyond that point, searching for the shapes of the cattle, and for Dog.

The afternoon sun glared on granite and sand, making it difficult to see. I nudged Shawnee forward a few paces, then shaded my eyes. There was a particular side canyon I was interested in because of a familiar coyote shape that crouched in the narrow throat of the arroyo.

"Now, why would he. . . ?" I mused aloud. A single cloud of no great size drifted obligingly across the sun. As the glare faded, the back wall of the box canyon jumped into high relief. Standing out against the granite walls were the dark forms of hundreds of cattle, milling about within the confines of the little valley and guarded by the patient watchfulness of Dog.

CHAPTER 19

I have heard it said that one of the cruelest tortures wrought upon a man is to deprive him of sleep for long periods of time. Tor and I had not allowed our eyes to close for almost forty-eight hours. While the others slept and worked in shifts, we dared not rest. The menacing thought of Jack Powers was always before us. How long did we have before Alzado reached Powers with the news of our approach? How long before Powers and his henchmen rode out to greet us? Although we were forced to depend on the remaining vaqueros, we dared not trust them.

By the light of our second campfire, the sleepless days and hours closed in on us.

"You're done up, Andrew," Tor said in a low voice as he sat beside me on a log.

"That I am." I could not argue. "And so are you, pard." Tor's eyes were ringed with dark circles. "You look like you've been hit in the face with a board."

He managed a faint smile. "You ain't gonna win no beauty prizes, neither." We both looked over our sleeping comrades with envy. Gomez and Ortiz stood watch over the herd now. Tor was set to join them, while I was to remain watchful here at the camp for two hours and then exchange places with Tor at midnight.

Tor rubbed his hand wearily over his eyes and gave his head a shake as if to clear away the grogginess. He muttered, "We ain't gonna be no use to nobody if'n we don't get some shut-eye. Why don't you sleep here a couple hours, Andrew? I'll wake you at the end of my watch, and you can take lookout while I sleep. Long as one or t'other of us is out with the herd and keepin' guard, it don't make no sense that t'other one of us can't rest a bit."

It was not so much the herd we were watching but the vaqueros. We both knew that. We trusted no one, even though we needed their help. Could it hurt if one of us slept for a bit as long as the other was alert?

In my muddled brain Tor's offer made sense. I nodded agreement, but I do not remember speaking to him. Sinking down, I let my head rest against the log. Tor dropped a tattered blanket on me, and I called Dog to come lie beside me. I closed my eyes with the knowledge that four-footed critters like Dog have some God-given sense that lets them be on guard even as they sleep. At the first whiff of danger my shaggy companion would alert me. One hand closed around the handle of my knife. The other rested on the ruff of Dog's neck. I was lost in profound sleep before Tor took his first step out of camp.

The sounds of the night mingled with my dreams. Far away I heard the night time bawling of cattle, and I dreamed myself riding among them. *I sat in my saddle. The Allen rifle was ready across my thighs. Shawnee moved effortlessly as I urged her around the perimeter. Then it was daylight, and somehow I was back in Santa Barbara on the Reed Rancho. Will Reed waved at me from where he rode on the far side of the herd. Peter was next to him on the curly-coated Chino. Sunlight glinted on his dark red hair, and he turned his face full toward me and smiled. I was relieved by this kindly sight of him, and I imagined that the stampede and the death of Peter had all been a nightmare! How good and true it seemed to be herding the cattle with the boy again! The nightmare of reality was turned around in my vision to become a vapor that I joyfully dismissed. "Buenos días, Peter!" I called, and I felt myself smile. There was no Alzado. No Gomez. No threat of Jack Powers or the lawless violence of the gold fields. . . .*

But suddenly the vision changed. I raised my eyes to see a rider approaching behind Peter. Dust rose like smoke from a vast fire behind the galloping bay. I strained to see who it was coming on so fast at Peter's back! A sense of dread filled me as I recognized the shape of Alzado, and then I saw him bring the Allen rifle up to his shoulder and take aim! I tried to shout a warning to Peter! I tried to call out the attacker's name! I reached for the Allen and realized with horror that I had given my rifle to Alzado! The fierce Yaqui now held Peter and me in the sights of my own gun!

"Look behind you!" I heard the cry.

Was it my voice shouting the alarm to Peter? Was

I calling for the boy to face the Indian?

I opened my mouth. No sound escaped. In that instant I realized that it was Alzado who was shouting. Not to Peter Reed, but to me! Peter dissolved in to a bloody, broken mass before my eyes!

"Look behind you, Señor Andrew!" screamed Alzado. "Turn! Turn! Open your eyes!"

I turned at his urging and saw the grinning face of Gomez on the hill behind me. Beside Gomez were the other vaqueros in a line. They parted, and Jack Powers rode out to lead them.

The earth rumbled, and I heard the low growl of Dog. I felt the warning of his snarl beneath my hand.

"Look behind you!" The voices of Peter and Alzado joined as one.

The dream erupted into reality as Dog leapt to his feet barking at the perimeter of the camp. My eyes snapped open.

"Look behind you!" shouted James Reed, tangled in his bedroll.

I scrambled for my Allen, then realized once again what was real and what was vision. Faces came into focus. I heard the hammer of a pistol click back and whirled to see the bloody form of Tor Fowler as he was shoved forward to fall at my feet. From the shadows, the grinning smirk of Gomez caught the firelight. He leveled his pistol at my gut, then waved it at the barred fangs of Dog.

"Do not shoot!" cried Joaquin. "You promised if I did not tell you would not kill —"

Gomez laughed at the boy and at the shocked look in my eyes.

"Did I say such a promise?"

Dog barked and made as if to lunge. "Dog!" I commanded, and with a gesture sent the animal back into the gloom of the brush. Gomez fired once, but I heard the chapparal cracking as Dog retreated. He had not been hit.

Tor lay in the dust and raised his head. "Andrew . . ." he moaned. "Sorry . . . pard . . . I dozed and they —" Ortiz kicked him hard in the belly, silencing him.

Gomez sneered more broadly as the other vaqueros joined him, holding each of the boys in their gun sights. Ramos had the look of a man ashamed. Ortiz and Sanchez took pleasure in our helplessness.

Joaquin clasped his hands together and dropped to his knees to beg for our lives. "I did as you told me, Gomez!" he wept. "I did not tell Señor Andrew!"

Ortiz leaned over and slapped the boy hard across the face, sending him sprawling back with a cry of pain.

"Enough!" I shouted. Gomez replied with a pistol shot aimed between my feet.

"You are in no position to say what is enough," Gomez replied with amusement. He smoothed his thin mustache and shoved his sombrero back on his head in a self-assured gesture. "You have never been in a position to say what was enough. That privilege has always been mine. Only you did not know it,

166

Señor Andrew." He bowed in a mocking way.

"Alzado?" I asked.

"The fierce Yaqui?" Gomez laughed. "A spineless coward, that one, mi amigo. He would not join us. I spoke to him early about our little business arrangement. He refused to be a part of it."

"And so it was you who cut his cinch."

Again the mocking bow and the smile that told everything. "A shame Don Peter got in the way. Ah, well. One less to worry about."

"Murderer!" Young John Reed lunged at Gomez as James tried to hold him back. With one blow, Sanchez knocked the boy unconscious to the ground.

"You are the leader of these children," Gomez said. "Silence them, or the next one will die." His fingers were white around the pistol grip. "I am growing weary of the game." He was not bluffing.

"Keep still," I issued the order quietly. A sense of my own foolishness filled me. I had been ready to lynch Alzado, who was the only man among seven vaqueros who had done no harm! Now the five who remained held guns to our bellies while Gomez painted the whole picture.

"This one," Gomez waved the gun at Tor, who remained unconscious. "Sí. A broken cinch? I have no taste for murder, you see. But a faulty cinch? What is that but carelessness? An accident. I can take no blame that he did not check. Accidents. I drop my gun and the herd stampeded. It was not I who caused Peter Reed to fall." He looked at James as the boy stared at him with unguarded hatred.

It was plain to me that in spite of his claims to not be a murderer, Gomez planned all along to murder us and take the herd. He had used us much in the way we had used him in order to move the herd close to the northern gold camps. Now our usefulness was at an end.

"You Americanos," he continued, "you steal all of California from us." He nodded toward his compatriots, and I knew this speech was meant for them as much as for us prisoners. "You steal the land. You steal the gold. You steal the cattle. No? Now we Californios take back the cattle. Just a few, señor." Gomez's face broke into a vermin's smile. "And then we will have a little of the gold, too. A small herd. Don Will Reed is a great man. He will hardly miss one thousand head, is this not so?"

"He will not care for a thousand head of cattle. . . . But if his sons are harmed, I know Don Will Reed will hunt you like a dog and see you hang for this," I replied. Then, glancing at the others, I added, "He will not rest until you are all dangling from an oak tree to rot at the end of a noose."

Such words had the effect I wished. The vaqueros looked fearfully at one another and then at Gomez. "I had nothing to do with the death of Peter Reed!" cried Ramos.

"We care only for the herd. For the gold," declared Ortiz gruffly. "We have nothing to do with the killing of men."

James cradled the head of his brother. "My father will see you all dead for what happened to Peter!" he cried.

"An accident!" Gomez spread his too-soft hands in protest. "I tell you it was no more than that! Meant to get Alzado out of the way!"

James opened his mouth as if to accuse again. I silenced the boy with a sharp look. Here was our only hope. "Sí," I agreed with Gomez. "Yes. No one can argue that. You meant no harm to poor Peter. An accident. You could not have known. Will Reed is a man of reason. For the lives of his sons and his friends, he would gladly offer you this ransom of one thousand beeves. What is that to him, Gomez? As long as we are set free. Unharmed." I directed my words to the other vaqueros who seized upon the lesser crime of rustling as though it was nothing compared to murder. What were a few cattle of a rich man, after all? Will Reed would not mind so much, would he? Not so long as James and John and Will Reed's friends were safe.

They began babbling at once to Gomez that they wanted no part in murder. Don Will Reed was a powerful man. He would not forgive harm done to his sons. The bandits united against the unspoken threat of our deaths. Gomez had lost the fight by his own argument that he was not a killer . . . merely a Californio patriot taking back what rightly belonged to other Californios!

I did not bring up the fact that the brigand he worked for was one of the American soldiers who had fought against the Californios with violence that defied description. No need to bring up the origins of Jack Powers now. Our captors somehow believed that they might escape justice by leaving us unharmed! The truth was that every last one of them would be hunted and captured and brought to justice. Inwardly I memorized the features of each face and the sound of each voice as I vowed that I would lead the hunt one day! For the time being, though, our lives were spared.

"I am no assassin, mi amigo," Gomez demurred again. He shrugged. "That is not to say I will not shoot out your knees if you resist me now." He motioned with the gun. "Sit down. Take your boots off." I obeyed, and he gestured broadly. "Yes. That's it. All of you. Take your boots off. Si. And the boots of Tor Fowler, if you please, señor?"

Our boots were thrust into a sack and tied to a horse. "Even used boots are worth something in the gold camp, I hear," Gomez laughed. "I shall sell them at a good price, to be sure."

After this he and his gang bound us tightly with leather thongs and then separated us, tying each of us to our own tree so that we could not help one another escape. Tor moaned and opened his eyes as Gomez mounted his horse and raised his arm in a rigid gesture of contempt.

"Hasta la vista, Americanos," Gomez laughed. "By the time you get free or are found, we will be rich men and long gone! Gracias, amigos! I shall think of you with amusement in days to come!"

Sunlight topped the jagged peaks of the Sierras as dust from the departing herd blended with the violet haze of dawn.

Chapter 20

I counted it a miracle that the five of us were still alive. But we were in need of another miracle — and soon. Trussed up like calves at a branding, barefoot and unarmed, there was no guarantee that we would not die here. I imagined some future traveler stumbling upon these five oak trees and five human skeletons grinning back.

My legs had no feeling below the knees. My fingers had gone numb right off, leaving it impossible for me to attempt to work the knot. No doubt the bandits had tied us with tourniquet-like tightness for this reason. What good would it do for us to have been left alive, only to die of starvation and thirst? Gomez, while claiming he was not a murderer, was killing us slowly by the same methods I had seen among the cruel Mojave Indians of the high desert. Left like this, we were dead men all the same without some help.

Tor came conscious and realized our predicament. I was at the top of the knoll, and he was at the bottom, facing the broad view of the valley. He could not see any of the rest of us. We were all scattered across the slope.

"Anybody there?" he called. A chorus of voices replied.

"Andrew."

"James."

"John."

And then a voice filled with remorse. "Joaquin."

"That's good," Tor's voice rang out. "Nice day, ain't it, Andrew?"

It was good to hear humor in Tor's voice. At least the thieves had not knocked that out of him.

"I've been sitting here thinking how glad I am it's not too hot," I shouted back.

"You're right on that score. I'm sittin' about a yard from a red anthill. On a hot day they'd be comin' out to take some sun and a piece of my hide, I reckon. Ain't but a few of the little beggars out on a day like this. They ain't got a whiff of me yet, neither."

I had also noticed a large anthill just spitting distance from my bare feet. In the cold morning air, the critters were barely moving. As the day warmed, I knew they would emerge a thousand strong. A moment later John called out that there was a colony to the right of where he was sitting, and James reported a nest of yellow jackets just above where he was tied. Joaquin said nothing at all, until I called to him.

"You got any mean little animals keeping you company, Joaquin?"

A long pause. "I wish I will die and all of you go free," he replied with such misery that I felt grieved for him. Then the explanation gushed from

172

him. "Gomez said he would not kill you if I did not tell what I heard him say about Jack Powers. He promised. That day I shot at you, it was because he pointed up and said 'Look quick, boy! There is the bandido Powers coming, shoot him quick!' And then I shot, and he slapped me. Later he said if I tell you, he will slit your throat in the night. But now we are tied like hogs and left for the ants to eat when the sun gets hot. I pray that I will suffer more. I pray that I will die and you all will get free before the day grows warm and the ants come awake! May God send His angels to set you free!" he cried.

I will admit that there are few things that make me more angry than a grown man who will threaten and bully a helpless animal, a woman, or a youngun. Gomez had not only shot at my dog, he had threatened and bullied a boy I had taken as my own. How many days and miles had young Joaquin carried the burden of terror that we would be massacred in our sleep if he spoke up about what he knew? And now, on top of it, he had the weight of a guilt that was too heavy for his young soul. This was more brutal than the sting of a whip for a child. Most younguns don't know that there's a big difference between a mistake in judgment and sin.

Tor spoke up a bit too cheerful for our situation. "Well, it ain't no mortal sin that you tried to keep us from gettin' our fool throats slit, boy. I ain't dead yet, and neither are you. I don't aim to be the main course in no red ant picnic, neither. How

173

'bout you, Andrew?"

"Nope." Then I added, "Don't let it trouble you, Joaquin. I'd of done the same." This last was true. I remembered clearly how at the age of twelve I had been bullied by a brigand who threatened the lives of those I loved most in the world. If we got free from this mess, I would tell Joaquin of my own experience at his age, and how a man had died because of my mistake. "Gomez won't get away with this. And you know I don't make idle promises."

No matter how brave I sounded, the thought came to me that maybe Gomez had gotten away with it and maybe I was making idle promises, after all. The sun rose higher, and the little mound of sand came alive with parades of red-worker ants, heading off to search for food.

My feet and calves were numb, and so I watched with a sort of detached horror as the first insect crawled out from between my big toe and my second toe. A horde followed, climbing the bottom of my foot and swarming through my toes like warriors breaching the top of a fortress wall. Tiny pinpricks of pain penetrated the numbness, and right before my eyes, my feet and ankles became a mass of bright red welts.

Moments after the first assault, John shouted that the ants near him were moving his way. James gave a sharp cry of pain, and we knew that he had been stung. The knoll, carefully chosen to provide a painful death for us, was coming alive.

I closed my eyes and prayed for some miracle

— some avenging angel to fly our way and set us free!

No avenging angel came with flaming sword to slice our bonds. Most times the Lord does not work that way. Miracles come as ordinary messengers. Ours came that day in the form of my half-coyote dog who trotted up the knoll and whined and wagged and licked my face. Behind him followed a stiff, cold breeze, and on the wind floated the first dark tide of rain clouds.

I cannot say what understanding the grinning stock dog had of our predicament, but he licked a row of ants off my right foot and then tugged at the rawhide reata that held my ankles.

"Yes!" I cried. "Good dog!" My praise disrupted him, and he stood and wagged and wandered up to lick my face. I inwardly upbraided myself, closed my eyes, and ignored him. Some other voice was speaking to his critter mind, and I knew I must not interfere with its instructions!

Another whine came as Dog sat down to consider me. With my hands bound behind my back and the reata encircling me and the tree, I was a curious sight in his yellow eyes. He licked my arm again, and then as his tongue rubbed over the rope, he paused, bumped against me, and then began to gnaw at the braided leather in earnest.

The sky darkened with the troop of storm clouds.

I heard Tor give a whoop of delight. "I felt a drop! By gum, Andrew! A raindrop!"

I dared not reply, for fear of breaking the intense

175

concentration of Dog. He was tugging and chewing the leather with the same enjoyment he might have gotten from a T-bone steak.

"Rain!" cried James.

"I felt it on my face!" shouted John. "Look there! The ants!"

No word came from Joaquin as those few light drops were joined by more and still more. I opened my eyes as the dry leaves rattled in the oak limbs above me. With pleasure I saw drops splash down on the frantic red horde as they scurried back toward the gravel hill like an army in retreat!

My red, swollen feet and ankles were washed clean of my tormentors! Thunder erupted, and lightning flashed just behind the mountain. Dog paused a moment, looked up, and then returned to his work as though his only aim in life was to chew through that tough hide rope!

"Andrew?" Tor called to me. "Andrew!" He demanded an answer.

"Shut up!" I shouted. Dog smiled at me and crunched his teeth, tugging as the leather frayed and weakened.

He seemed to be wondering why I did not help him? Could I not fight against the loop and break free? his look asked me. My arms were bloodless, dead. It would take me a while to move, I knew, even when I was loose from this hold.

I leaned my head back against the rough trunk of my prison and squeezed my eyes tight. I prayed as I had not prayed before in my life! The raindrops broke with the thunder into a downpour, clattering through the branches, drenching me and my fur-covered angel. The rawhide dampened. Dog tugged harder, chewed more fervently, pulled back in a tug of war until the reata yielded at last with a sharp snap.

With a cry, I toppled over in the mud. My hands and ankles were still bound with leather strips. Dog stood over me, nosing me as if to ask why I did not stand.

"Tor!" I shouted after another thunderclap. "Dog has chewed away the reata! I can't move. Got no feeling in my arms or legs."

Another crash of thunder drowned out his exultant reply. I lay on my side and eyed a small rain puddle forming as my arms and legs began the excruciating ache of rushing blood. And now the fire of the ant bites took hold. I gasped and groaned. Dog patiently licked my wounds and waited.

The heaviness of my limbs dissipated, and I suddenly felt the soothing coldness of the rain and the roughness of Dog's tongue. I moved my legs and scooted toward the mud puddle. Thrusting my hands and wrists into the mire, I began to work the leather. It stretched, it swelled with moisture, at last it yielded, and my hands slipped free!

With fumbling fingers I worked the knots of rawhide at my ankles. Then I grasped the trunk of the oak and managed to pull myself erect on unsteady legs. A moment more of agony broke as the full force of sensation flooded back. Then I raised my eyes gratefully heavenward and knew that what was just a sudden squall for another man was my miracle! What might be a hungry dog chewing through leather, to someone else's thinking, was for me the mighty hand of the Lord!

I stumbled down to unloose Tor. Then I raced to free Joaquin, who was bound with my black bullwhip! James and John half-crawled, half-stumbled to us. We all embraced. We cheered Dog and thanked heaven for the rain, and then we helped one another to the mint patch by the creek bed to doctor our ant bites.

CHAPTER 21

Cold water from the stream and crushed mint leaves did something to soothe the searing sting of our bites. But there was no remedy to cool the burning anger we each felt toward the men who had deceived us and left us to die.

Still, I felt the obligation for the safety of the Reed brothers and for young Joaquin. We were without weapons and on foot. What chance would two men and three boys have against five armed vaqueros with a talent for ruthless cruelty?

The settlement called Tuleberg was several days' hike from where we were stranded. We would take the boys there for safety, and then Tor and I could set out alone to track Gomez. I laid out this plan to the boys as we rigged makeshift moccasins out of a discarded cowhide and a torn saddle blanket left behind by the gang.

James Reed raised his chin proudly, and I saw the determination of his father burning in his eyes. "If we go to Tuleberg, we will lose the herd."

" 'Peers to me we already lost the herd, boy," Tor said, sucking on a mint leaf and rubbing his legs.

James turned on Tor angrily. "They killed Peter. Stole my father's cattle. Left us to die! By some miracle we are not only alive, but well and strong —"

"And angry," added young John. "I could not look Father in the eye again if we let them get away with this!"

"You youngsters don't understand, it seems to me —" Tor began, only to be savagely interrupted by the fury of James Reed.

"No! It is you who do not understand! We can beat them!"

"They have our guns," I tried to calm the boy. "Our horses."

"We have more than they would have if they were an army with cannons!" James cried with clenched fists.

Tor and I exchanged doubtful looks. "James —"

"We are stronger than they!" said Joaquin, joining against our better judgment.

"Yes! Stronger!" John leapt to his feet. "They cannot win! Will not win!"

"We are unarmed," Tor argued. "I don't aim to take you boys home to your mama in a sack, and that's final."

James narrowed his eyes and considered Tor for a moment. "You are a coward, Tor Fowler!" he said in a level voice. This was a foolish thing to say to Tor. I have known the mountain man to knock the teeth out of a man for a lot less than those words.

"Whoa up there, James," I said.

Then the boy turned on me. "And you are a coward, Andrew Sinnickson! And you spit in the

180

eye of God if we do not go after Gomez and the others!"

"Spit in the eye!" Tor declared, puffing up like a bullfrog. "Why you little whelp pup! I ought to —"

"He is right, Señor Tor," Joaquin leapt into the fray. "Angels bring the rain to save us! Dog, who is a smart dog, but all the same he is still a dog . . . he chews through the rope! We are free. It is a miracle. Any priest will say it is so. Now you want to run away."

"Not run," I fumed. "Get you boys safe, that's all."

"It is our fight as much . . . no . . . more than yours!" James insisted. "It is my brother who lies buried in Mariposa." He fished a rumpled paper from his pocket and unfolded it to reveal a page from my Bible. "I found this," James held the page up. "I took it for a sign. For a promise." He began to read the words from the fragment. " 'Who hath any strength, except our God? It is God, that girdeth me with strength of war.' " He looked up. "It's torn there, but see the rest of it." He gave it to me to read.

I studied the ragged slip a moment and then read aloud what remained. " 'He teacheth my hands to fight: and my arms shall break even a bow of steel. Thou hast given me the defense of thy salvation: thy right hand shall hold me up. Thou shalt make room enough under me for to go: that my footsteps shall not slide.' " I swallowed hard and then finished the verse. " 'I will follow upon my enemies, and overtake them: neither will I turn again till I have destroyed them.' "

It was here that the page was torn away. I passed the fragment to Tor who reread the words silently as James Reed stared me down like the shepherd boy David must have shamed the men who said no one could beat Goliath.

"Well, then." Tor blinked at me and then looked at James in a new light. "I'll be . . ."

"They're just men," James replied firmly. "And dark sinners at that. What hope do they have when they're in the wrong? And how can we turn away when we're in the right? I got to tell you. If I strike out from this place alone, I'm going to do it! There it is . . . *the word*. Isn't it? You think it's just an accident I found that? The rain and the dog? Just coincidence? Right is right and wrong is wrong. And there's a God who knows the difference. Father always taught us boys that this was true."

"That's right," agreed John.

"So you go to Tuleberg if you want," James said, putting his arms around the shoulders of Joaquin and John. "We three are striking out to take back what's ours. If we do not, then no honest man in all of California will be safe! We stop it here, or there will be no stopping it!"

It would have been easy enough I suppose for Tor and me to wallop the lot of them, tie them up, and drag them to safety, but the truth was that we two grown men were shamed and instructed by what they said. Two unarmed men and three boys taking back eight hundred head of cattle from an armed gang would be some sort of warning to others who might try murdering and stealing over honest employment . . . if we did indeed succeed in such a desperate gamble. Could I now discount what I had considered a miracle when I was set free? Could I doubt that some kind force was watching over us? Helping us when we were helpless, yet expecting us to also do our part in the drama?

These were matters far beyond my understanding and my ability to wholly believe. And yet I knew that what James said was true. Right was right and wrong was wrong. Deep down I felt that the battle of Good and Evil was an ancient war fought in the fields of men's eternal souls. Many times evil triumphed simply because good men backed down or turned away or gave up in the face of difficult odds. James Reed did not say all these things out loud, and yet I heard them as clearly as if the boy had preached a sermon. He, like a young shepherd boy named David, was willing to face what I perceived to be a Goliath simply because he believed unshakably that Good must prevail over Evil.

James retrieved the thin leaf of paper from Tor and returned it to his breast pocket. "If I am killed, Señor Andrew," he leveled his green eyes on me, "take this to my father. Tell him I died believing this. Tell him I fought like a man." He turned his gaze to the hills. "I could never go home and tell him I ran away from the men who killed Peter."

Chapter 22

The owl hoot was low and mournful sounding. Its aching tone brought to my mind a hollowed-out old snag of an oak that stood on the bluff above the Cherokee camp where I grew up. There had been a great horned owl who lived in that snag. Its call had been a beacon from far across the prairie.

The difference was, this night owl I knew by name. It was Tor Fowler, and the signal meant that he was in position.

That we had caught up to the rustlers in one day and half a night had more to do with good fortune and Divine Providence than how fleet-footed we were. Truth to tell, our feet were sore, and only periodic stops to reline our improvised moccasins with moss and crushed mint leaves kept us going.

When I had spotted the herd from the tall pinnacle, I had not only seen the box canyon, but had located another feature of interest as well. This second observation I had not shared with anyone until after the theft of the herd.

It seems that the wandering course of the stream bed and the track by which the cattle would be moved curved around the range of hills. By hard hiking and climbing, we five were able to cross the narrow range and traverse in three miles what the herd would cover in ten.

That still left us miles behind, but we never slackened our pace. We knew that with only five vaqueros to handle eight hundred head, they would not be moving any too fast.

We were right. By midnight we were close enough to see the glow of their campfire. At three in the morning by the set of the stars, we were almost ready.

The biggest worry in our plan was right at the beginning. A loud yell or a gunshot fired by either of the two sentries would bring the other three boiling out of their camp. Their pistols would be too much for our fists unless we could even the score some first. "The problem," as Tor phrased it as we had hiked and plotted, "is how to separate two snakes from their fangs without waking up the rest of a nest of vipers."

On the far side of the grassy plain, Tor, James Reed and Dog were watching the movements of a night herder. Even though I could not see what was happening with Tor, I watched it unfold in my mind's eye. A hand signal from Tor sent Dog across in front of the guard, close enough to be momentarily in sight, but not so close that the vaquero could be sure of what he had seen.

If it worked, the sentry's attention would be focused on the place where a gray spotted shape had appeared and disappeared. Tor would be creeping up behind, readying himself for what came next.

I motioned for John and Joaquin to stop the moment I picked up the outline of the vaquero on our side of the herd. He was less than thirty yards away; and what was more, from the white patches that stood out against the shadow, he had drawn Shawnee from the string as his mount.

I gave a deep owl call of reply that meant we were also ready. Now it was up to our prayers and the resolve to not draw back once it started.

Shawnee's ears had no doubt been pricking back and forth ever since the first owl hoot. As an old Indian fighter herself, she would know what was afoot.

I moved up so as to keep a sleepy black steer between me and the guard. When the animal moved closer, so did I. Just when I was congratulating myself on how well things were going, the wayward critter abruptly turned off the wrong way, leaving me hanging out like a shirt on a clothesline.

I dropped flat on my belly behind a clump of brush. After a moment, I started to inch my way forward, but a bunch of dead weeds crackled under me. The vaquero turned his head at the sound, and I ducked my face so there could be no reflection off my eyes.

The sweat broke out on my forehead, despite the coolness of the night and the damp grass. One shout, one shot, and all would be lost. If we were caught this time, there would be no second chance — not even an anthill — just five dead bodies left for the buzzards.

Another steer ambled by, actually stepping over me as it grazed. As I held my breath, fearful that it would tread right on me, it too broke through the brush with a rattle and a snap.

No gunshot came and no call of alarm. The vaquero must have decided that the steer had made both noises. When I chanced a peek again, he was facing away from me into the dark.

I thought I heard a muffled thud and the sound of hooves from away off on the other side of the drove, but it could not matter now. It was time to get this show on the road.

Slowly and quietly, making no noise, I stood up. I shook out the coil of my whip. If Shawnee knew I was there, she gave no sign, giving me the only chance I would have. My first cast would have to be perfect.

In the dark it was hard to judge distances. I slipped a little closer then a little closer yet.

Now! The whip flicked out, but instead of slashing the vaquero's back, it knotted around his throat. It is human nature that when something grabs you by the neck, your hands instinctively fly upward to try to clear the stranglehold away.

That is exactly what the night herder did. As his grip left the reins to reach for what was choking him, I gave a sudden yank, and Shawnee spurted forward. Remember, he was riding bareback with just a blanket under him. The guard slid off backward like a watermelon seed squirting between your fingers.

By the time he hit the ground, I was on top

of him. It was Sanchez. He was dazed from the impact and still trying to uncoil the lash from around his gullet. His eyes went wide when he saw me, but the right I threw at his chin from two feet away laid him out cold.

A low "hist" from me brought the boys to my side. We stuffed Sanchez's mouth with rags, then trussed him up with my whip. The pistol had been knocked from his belt by the fall, but John and Joaquin scoured the clumps of grass until they located it.

Another crackle in the brush made me whirl around, pistol in hand, but it was only Tor with James and Dog. They were leading a lineback dun.

"How'd it go?" I whispered.

"Like a charm!" Tor's hoarse reply was all smiles. "It was Garcia. Dog got his attention, and I give the Paiute rush. I taken him clean off the horse while it was between one mouthful of grass and the next. He hit the ground without never havin' a chance to draw, nor call out. 'Course," he said without remorse, "I think his neck is broke. Anyways, he ain't movin'."

Tor and I sat our mounts and waited in the chilly dark. I was grateful that the serape I had taken from Sanchez was both disguising and warming. We were waiting for the stars to swing round. Too early and Gomez would know something was wrong.

When it was time, I grasped Fowler by the hand. "I'm glad to have you," I said.

Tor's reply was grimly humorous. "Thunder-ation, Andrew! I wouldn't miss this show for all the gold in the Calaveras."

We separated then, one to either end of the camp. We left the three boys and Dog to guard Sanchez.

I held the pistol low across my chest behind the serape and moved Shawnee into a slow walk, directly toward the fire. I needed a chance to locate all three men if I could. These bandidos weren't dumb; even if they did not expect to be attacked, they still slept back in the shadows and not up close where the firelight would pinpoint their whereabouts.

I saw Gomez first. He was the one closest to the warmth, which seemed right in character to me. Over on the right, underneath the low-hanging branches of a fir tree was another, but whether Ortiz or Ramos, I could not tell.

Gomez stirred and rolled over. I knew that as he came awake he would be thinking, "What time is it?" and "Is it the end of the watch?" I adjusted Sanchez's sombrero lower to shield my face and cocked the hammer of the pistol.

Sitting up and rubbing sleep from his eyes, Gomez heard the sound of Shawnee's hooves and reached for his gun. Catching sight of the familiar serape relaxed him, and he called out, "Hola, San-chez? Qué hora es? What is the time?"

Where was the third man? In just a few seconds the ball would open and the location of the missing dance partner was important.

"Qué ocurre? What is it, Sanchez? Is anything wrong?"

It was time. I could only hope that Fowler had been able to pick up the last outlaw's location from his different vantage point.

I drew the pistol and tipped back the sombrero. "Freeze, Gomez!" I ordered.

His hand started to move toward the weapon, and then he stopped. A momentary anger was replaced by a grin as he sized up the situation. "You have made a losing bet, señor," he said. "You are here alone and we are three."

"I don't think this wager was so bad," I said calmly. "Listen carefully, Gomez. Raise your hands over your head. Then tell your friends in the brush to do the same."

The familiar smirk was back. "Why would I do that, gringo? Right now you are surrounded."

"Because whatever happens, you are going to die," I replied. "Do you really think I won't blow your head off from this distance? It doesn't matter who shoots first, because you'll be just as dead."

I was near enough to see his throat work as he thought this over, and then he said, "Ortiz, don't do anything stupid."

Clearly he was hoping that the remaining unseen gunman would circle and get the drop on me. Was he right?

Out of the dark and off to my left came a familiar throaty chuckle. "It's okay, Andrew," Tor's voice called. "I got Ramos. Caught him with his pants down, so to speak."

That's when Ortiz decided to make his play. I caught a movement out of the corner of my eye, and the pistol bucked in my hand as I snapped a shot into the thickest shadow under the fir branches.

I heard Ortiz yell, and then Gomez was going for his gun. The muzzle was turning my way, the barrel pivoting up as I whipped my sights back around and fired.

Gomez was overeager. He shot before he aimed, and his bullet went through the broad brim of the sombrero I wore. I don't know where my slug caught him, but he fired only the one time.

I slid off Shawnee and divided my attention between Gomez and the brush where Ortiz lay. Tor marched Ramos into camp and roughly ordered him to sprawl on his face by the fire. With me covering, Fowler checked the other two and announced that they were both dead.

"Well, pard," he said, "looks like we got us a herd again."

CHAPTER 23

Three more graves beside the trail greeted the dawn below Sierran skies. Sanchez had his hands tied behind his back, and I had my whip coiled and hanging again at my side.

Tor and I had a serious discussion with Ramos. He seemed the least hardened of all the outlaws, and we surely needed help with the herd. In the end we compromised. We gave him his parole in order to gain a sixth drover to our band, but we kept his gun and knife.

The dewdrops sparkled on the milkweed, and the morning brightened into what we hoped would be one of the last few days on the trail. "Head 'em out, James," I called. The boys, who had done the work of men and seen trouble and shown courage and resolve beyond their years, set the herd on the move.

We made Sanchez walk. Aside from being a rough kind of justice, it gave us little need to watch him. Besides, he had the most watchful of all possible guards. We set Dog to keep an eye on him, and you can believe that a meaningful growl and the flash of white teeth gave the outlaw plenty of mind to keep up and not stray.

The day passed without incident. We moved the

cattle slowly, keeping them bunched so as to not make more work for ourselves. The herd had been pushed into a narrow place between two low ranges of hills. The trail followed the watershed and curved around to the north about a half mile ahead of where I rode the drag spot.

I was thinking that even eating trail dust felt good after all we'd been through, and even better since it would soon be done. Up ahead the steers were starting to bunch up and mill around. The leaders had stopped for some unknown reason, as though they had run into a wall just around the bend.

I kicked Shawnee into her ground-eating canter. I had been woolgathering for so long that I'd lost track of Tor and James, who should have been just ahead of me and on either side.

It was too early to halt for the night. Through my mind went thoughts of high water across the trail or an encounter with a grizzly, but there was no serious concern in me.

So I was completely unprepared when Shawnee and I loped around the corner and ran smack spraddle into Jack Powers. Flanking him were Ed and Patrick Dunn.

My move to draw Sanchez's pistol was stopped when I saw that Patrick Dunn was holding Joaquin off the ground under one arm. Ed held a rifle on Tor, Ramos, and the Reed brothers, while a grinning Sanchez collected our pistols. Dog had run off again.

I yanked Shawnee to a savage halt, setting her

haunches down. "Let him go," I growled at Pat.

It was Powers who answered. "Not so fast, Sinnickson. Tell me, who is holding all the cards this time?"

"I've got ten men with rifles coming up pronto," I bluffed. "If you know what's good for you, you better light out quick and not mess with us."

Powers laughed until his eyes ran a stream of tears past the red bulb of his nose. And what could I do, while Dunn held on to Joaquin?

"Ten men with rifles, you say? That's rich! I say this sorry band of dog meat is everybody. What you've got is a broken-down mountain goat, a traitor, and three cubs that should have been drowned at birth. Rodriguez has been watching you since noon — we just didn't want to scatter the herd, so we waited until now to collect you."

He was so sure of himself it made my blood boil. From behind a boulder rode Rodriguez, the vaquero who had disappeared after the snake episode long before. He also had a rifle across the withers of the palomino. "Greetings, señor!" he said with mocking cheerfulness. "How pleasant to see you again. Where is my good friend Gomez and the others? I thought to meet *them*, but we were not expecting *you*."

"Gomez is dead," I said coldly. "So are Garcia and Ortiz. You sure you're on the winning side, Rodriguez?"

"Enough of this pointless jabber," Powers interrupted. "Drop your gun and get over with the others. Pat, throw down the kid. That's the lot

194

of them, except the dog."

We six, since they intended to kill Ramos along with us, were herded into a small group. Facing us were four men with rifles in their hands and greed and murder in their hearts. "Gold on the hoof," Powers said, marveling at the size of the drove. "All right, let's get on with it."

A rifle shot from the ridge line back of me split the afternoon stillness. The slug hit the ground right between the front feet of Powers' buckskin. The animal jerked and danced, bumping into the other mounts while the outlaws nervously tried to regain control. Patrick raised his rifle to meet the unexpected threat and was cautioned by these words. "Stand easy, boys," said a nasally, Yankee-fied voice. "That was just to get your attention."

It was Ames. Beside him with a smoking Allen rifle stood Alzado. Hulking nearby was the grizzly bear figure of Boki, and as if this weren't enough, Dog was wagging among two hundred Angel's Camp miners.

"There's your beef, boys," Ames said. "Just like I promised."

Whooping and hollering so that I thought the herd might turn and hightail it back to southern California, the troop of hungry prospectors charged down the hillside, surrounding both us and Powers' men.

Tor went up to Powers and demanded that the outlaw chief get off his horse. Tor proceeded to explain exactly what was going to happen to the bandit when he did so.

Powers shook his head and waved the rifle. "What's the matter, mountain man? Can't you take a joke? Why, all we did was ride out to meet you same as these others. I wanted to make an offer to buy your herd, not knowing it was a spoken for."

"Why you . . ."

I thought for an instant that Tor would do his Paiute trick right there on Powers, but the would-be rustler and murderer spoke quickly. "Easy there, mountain man. If you want to start a war, remember we've still got our rifles. Besides, a whole lot of innocent people might get hurt."

"He's right, Tor," I said reluctantly. "Let him go."

"But he . . . this . . . lowdown . . ."

Words failed my friend, and I have to admit that I didn't like it either, but for once, Powers was right. The cheering, celebrating miners scarcely noticed when a sullen file of riders, led by Jack Powers, exited up the canyon and out of sight.

CHAPTER 24

Never try to tell me that the Almighty does not have a sense of humor. After all the tragedy and triumph of weeks on the drive, you would think that a period of rest and relaxation would follow.

Rest, yes. Relaxation, ha!

Three days after we got to Angel's Camp, we had tidied up the details of the sale. All tolled, the cattle brought in some eighty thousand dollars worth of dust, nuggets, and the three-ounce gold slugs called "adobes." And then I got sick.

Not anything life-threatening, like cholera, or dramatic, like pneumonia. No sir, I couldn't even get sympathy. I came down with the mumps.

The doctor gave me a mess of willow bark tea and a bandage to wrap around my swollen jaws. When I asked him what else to do, he scratched his head and said, "Ache some, I guess. You'll be better in a week or two."

He was right, but the trouble was, the rest of my party couldn't wait. You see, Powers was still a force to be reckoned with, especially with so much gold at stake. So we had gratefully accepted the offer to journey south with a company of United States infantry.

The lieutenant of that detail, a young man with

the imposing name of William Tecumsah Sherman, set the departure date. When it was time to leave, I was still a week or so from being well enough to travel.

Tor, Joaquin, and the Reeds had come to tell me goodbye. It was not a tearful farewell. Truth to tell, they mostly stood way back and laughed at my cheeks.

"I'm powerful sorry, Andrew," Tor said. (He didn't look sorry.) "We'll see your share safe to Santa Barbara and meet up with you there in another ten days or so."

"Just you leave me a thousand of my share," I instructed, "and you won't see me for a month. I've a mind to see San Francisco before I head south. You can start the next roundup, and then I'll join you."

So, a few days after that parting, Dog, Shawnee, and I were finally on the trail. I was headed down the same Calaveras path I had ridden up a few months before. It seemed both a short while and long ages since I had seen it last.

The road had been widened and improved some to accommodate Ames's supply wagons and the tracks of some thousand eager miners who had come after us. I could still recognize the original landmarks though, like the creek bottom where the Indians had been attacked and the precipice where Ames had almost been killed.

When my casual inspection took in the top of the cliff where the rock slide had started, I almost dropped my teeth. I thought I saw the glint of light on metal in the same spot as we were ambushed before. Just a quick flash and nothing to follow, but it took me aback enough that I called Dog to me and looked things over in earnest. I even pulled my brand-new Colt repeating rifle from its boot.

Well, after watching a while, and not remarking another sign, I put it down to the aftereffects of my sickness and nudged Shawnee forward. We were well on down the trail when some distance ahead I saw a mounted man blocking the road with rifle in hand.

It was too far to say if it really was Patrick Dunn. But when I halted and looked over my shoulder, I saw a similarly armed rider closing in behind me. This second fellow looked like Pat's brother Ed.

You know, I hate coincidences. I turned Shawnee to the side, dashed down a short slope and splashed across the creek. Once on the other side, I set her up the incline at a dead run. I had just reached a clump of rocks at the summit when a gunshot from the *far* side of the hill told me that I had ridden right into their trap. I pulled up by the rocks, flung myself down and settled in to watch a bit.

I did not have long to wait. A second bullet smashed into a boulder near my head and scattered rock fragments all around. I fired a blast to make him keep his head down for a second and was gratified to hear a yelp of pain. I yanked the saddlebags off Shawnee and slapped her into a run across the grade. Dog and I ducked back under cover.

Three riders crossed the creek below me. It was the two Dunns and a dark-complected, rough-looking character. This last man shouted, "There's his horse!"

Patrick Dunn yelled back, "Let it go! It's Sinnickson we want!"

I snapped off a quick shot and rolled to a new position as the return fire came in. I heard Pat shouting, "Ed! Ed!"

So I'd accounted for Ed Dunn. But how many more were there, and what was their plan? Another shot splintered the tree bark just back of me and reminded me just how bad things were.

"Sinnickson!" a bellowing voice raged. "Sinnickson, do you hear me?" Patrick Dunn screamed at me again, "Sinnickson, I'm going to butcher you! You killed Ed, and I'm going to cut out your heart and feed it to you!"

I knew better than to make any reply, since any sound would draw a shot. All I could do now was wait for one of them to make a false move. By keeping still, I was able to wing the dark-complected killer, but then things settled into a stalemate of sorts. I kept wishing that someone from the Angel's Camp road might come to see what the shooting was about, but in those lawless times, I knew this to be a vain hope.

Sundown would finish me. If a ricochet had not struck me first, the cover of darkness would let them move up close enough to fire directly into my hiding place.

"Sinnickson!" Jack Powers' voice this time, trying to work on my nerves. "Johns here says he's going to skin your dog. Says he owes the dog one from last summer!"

I don't know why, but that was the point at which I gave up despair and began to hope again. Somehow, the humorous idea of that Johns fellow holding a grudge against Dog for ripping the seat out of his britches; well, it just struck me funny, and I knew everything would work out, some way.

It wasn't full dark in the west, but the stars were filling up the eastern sky. I figured the rush was coming most any time, and I needlessly checked the load of the rifle again.

One star directly east of me seemed especially bright. In fact, it appeared much brighter than usual. As I studied it for a while, it looked to be growing larger and larger.

I was so fascinated, I almost forgot to duck when the bullets started flying. Dog and I ducked back successfully again, and I squeezed off a few rounds to let them know I wasn't done yet.

When I glanced eastward again, the star had visibly grown. It was now plainly a fireball in the sky, and it was headed straight for me! There was a fearful roaring noise overhead; then the sky all around blazed with sudden light. A rushing hot wind that accompanied the shooting star blasted through the trees, and the tops of several pines burst into flames. A second later there was a fearsome impact, as if two buffalo the size of mountain peaks had collided head-on.

The whole hillside shook with force. Boulders bounced around me, one clipping Dog with a glancing blow. Trees toppled like matchsticks, and a jumble of them exploded into a fire that swept the bottom of the hill on the wings of that strange, unnatural wind.

Through the dancing flames I could see my enemies jumping and running toward the creek to escape the conflagration. One of them shook his fist in my direction, but whether the gesture was meant for me or Almighty God, I could not say.

A few minutes later, Dog and I crossed the bare peak and descended the reverse slope. The body of the man I had shot earlier lay where he had fallen, unmindful of the inferno raging just on the other side of the hill. I whistled up Shawnee, and we rode out of the River of the Skulls.

EPILOGUE

It was some six months later that I returned to the Calaveras country. After the winter snows had melted and the river crossings had become manageable, Tor and I pushed another herd of a thousand head up to the hungry miners.

If the second drive lacked the adventure of the first, it was also minus the tragedy. Will Reed's vaqueros had returned from trying their hand at prospecting, and there was no shortage of reliable help. By the way, Will and Francesca's child arrived — a red-haired boy that they named Simon.

The charred remains of a whole hillside made locating the spot of the ambush easy. There was even a pattern to the way the oaks and firs had tumbled down that sort of pointed me back to the meteor's impact.

I had a real worshipful feeling as I walked Shawnee slowly over the ground. I went there with the intention of saying a few words of thanks, and this I did.

The crater on the muddy hillside had already started to erode from the runoff of the melting snow. Shawnee was headed back toward Angel's Camp road when something caught my eye.

Washed clean of the clay and standing out against the backdrop of a quartz ledge was a black, fist-shaped chunk of rock. I knew it immediately for what it was: a piece of a shooting star.

But it was more. This misshapen lump of iron was a flaming messenger with a fiery sword sent by the hand of God. I have kept it with me ever since.

The employees of G.K. HALL hope you have enjoyed this Large Print book. All our Large Print titles are designed for easy reading, and all our books are made to last. Other G.K. Hall Large Print books are available at your library, through selected bookstores, or directly from us. For more information about current and upcoming titles, please call or mail your name and address to:

G.K. HALL
PO Box 159
Thorndike, Maine 04986
800/223-6121
207/948-2962